# The Canterbury Tales

First published in 2008 by Usborne Publishing Ltd,
Usborne House, 83-85 Saffron Hill, London
EC1N 8RT, England.
www.usborne.com

Copyright © 2008 Usborne Publishing Ltd.

The name Usborne and the devices ♛ ⊕ are
Trade Marks of Usborne Publishing Ltd.

All rights reserved. No part of this publication may be
reproduced, stored in a retrieval system or transmitted
in any form or by any means, electronic, mechanical,
photocopying, recording or otherwise, without
the prior permission of the publisher.

JFMAMJJ SOND/23 00350/20

ISBN 9780746099308

Printed and bound by CPI (UK) Ltd, Croydon CR0 4YY

Designed by Brenda Cole
Series editor: Jane Chisholm
Series designer: Mary Cartwright
Cover illustration and design by Candice Whatmore
Cover background manuscript: Huntington Library and Art Gallery,
San Marino, CA, USA / The Bridgeman Art Library

# The Canterbury Tales

From the story by
## Geoffrey Chaucer

Retold by Sarah Courtauld,
Dr. Abigail Wheatley & Susanna Davidson

Illustrated by Ian McNee

# Contents

About the Canterbury Tales     7

The Prologue     10
(about the Canterbury Pilgrims)

The Knight's Tale     22
(about Palamon and Arcite who both loved Emily)

The Miller's Tale     36
(about John the Carpenter and the End of the World)

The Reeve's Tale     49
(about Surly Simpkin, Frightful Fanny and Miserable Molly)

The Man of Law's Tale     57
(about Constance and her Perilous Voyages)

The Wife of Bath's Tale     72
(about a Knight and a Loathly Lady)

The Friar's Tale     81
(about a Man who went to the Devil)

The Merchant's Tale     89
(about Love, Marriage and Pear Trees)

## The Squire's Tale     98
(about the Five Magic Gifts)

## The Franklin's Tale     105
(about a Knight, a Fair Lady and a Magician)

## The Pardoner's Tale     115
(about Death and the Three Wastrels)

## Chaucer's Tale     122
(about Sir Topaz and the Giant)

## The Nun's Priest's Tale     127
(about a Fox and some Chickens)

## The Canon's Yeoman's Tale     137
(about a Wicked Alchemist)

## The Manciple's Tale     146
(about Apollo and the White Crow)

## The Epilogue     152
(about Why there aren't any more Tales)

## About Geoffrey Chaucer     156

# About the Canterbury Tales

For many people, Chaucer's *Canterbury Tales* marks the start of modern English literature. Outrageous, comic and thought-provoking, the stories and characters provide all kinds of intriguing insights into life, love and insult-flinging in medieval England. But perhaps most importantly, Geoffrey Chaucer wrote in English at a time when many people in England were reading, writing and talking mainly in Latin and French. This heralded a swing back to English that has never faltered since. So *The Canterbury Tales* is the earliest English writing that many people read.

Geoffrey Chaucer was a witty and observant 14th-century Londoner, whose work took him on frequent journeys and introduced him to people from all walks of life and professions. These experiences inspired him to write a series of funny – and sometimes shocking – stories, poems and anecdotes, which he worked on for at least ten years of his life.

The idea behind the *Tales* is simple: an ill-matched group of people set off on horseback on a religious pilgrimage from London to visit the shrine of St. Thomas in Canterbury Cathedral. They agree that each of them will tell stories to pass the time along the way. Chaucer describes each of the pilgrims and records some of their banter, as well as their tales. He also includes himself in the group as a comic figure: an overweight, bumbling poet whose verse is so bad that he is quickly silenced by the other pilgrims. But his funny, cutting comments and the varied, lively tales reveal his true skill and subtlety as a writer.

Chaucer wrote in the days long before printing, when books were written out laboriously by hand – which meant they were very expensive and hard to come by. Even so, *The Canterbury Tales* quickly became the medieval equivalent of a bestseller.

Part of its appeal was the fact that Chaucer wrote in English rather than Latin or French – this was a new and exciting idea at the time. His characters were unusual too. While other authors focused on heroes, kings and saints from history, Chaucer chose quirky individuals who were typical of his own time. Some were even based on real people: Harry Bailey actually owned an inn in Southwark, and Roger the Cook was also a genuine medieval Londoner.

So, *The Canterbury Tales* made a refreshing change for medieval readers. But, like many other writers of his time, Chaucer often preferred to write in poetry, so most of the original *Tales* were presented in verse. To make things easier for modern readers, this re-telling uses only a little verse, and it also shortens many of the tales and tidies up some of the loose ends that Chaucer left hanging.

## About the Canterbury Tales

There are many things about *The Canterbury Tales* that still puzzle experts to this day. Chaucer's Prologue suggests that each pilgrim would tell four tales. But Chaucer only wrote a fraction of this number, and some of the pilgrims he describes don't have a tale at all. Chaucer never mentions when, or even if, the pilgrims arrive in Canterbury, nor does he give any details about the journey back to London. Many of the tales trail off without proper endings, or seem to be interrupted. Some experts think Chaucer never finished the *Tales* at all.

Even so, he had a lasting influence on British writers. Over 200 years later, Shakespeare read Chaucer's work and even based one of his plays, *Troilus and Cressida*, on a poem by Chaucer. And Shakespeare wasn't the only one. Even today, many writers and readers are inspired by the freshness, wit and energy of *The Canterbury Tales*.

# The Prologue
(about the Canterbury Pilgrims)

Everything was sun-drenched, rain-bathed, springing into life. Tender green shoots burst from the ground, the west wind blew its sweet breath and every tree and bush I passed was alive with bird song. I could feel it was springtime in my bones. It was the right time for travel, for adventure, for brave pilgrimages to strange and distant lands...

I wasn't going quite that far though: just from London to Canterbury, where the great saint, Thomas Becket, lies. I was on the road to Southwark and the bustling Tabard Inn – my journey's starting point.

I stabled my horse, pushed open the inn door, and promptly staggered backwards at the smell. After the fresh air outside, I was quite unprepared for the stench of onions, sweat and ale mixed with wood-smoke from the fire.

"Welcome!" roared a voice, and the innkeeper, Harry Bailey, clapped a huge, plate-sized hand on my shoulder. "Well, well, Geoffrey Chaucer, the famous writer," he said, his blue eyes bulging close to mine, "it's good to see you again. Making a pilgrimage are you? You're in good company! Look around the room. There are about twenty other folk here for the same reason."

I nodded vaguely at Harry. He was a good soul, but I had my reasons for keeping quiet about the real purpose of my journey. As my eyes grew accustomed to the fug, I looked around for a place to sit – but every bench seemed bursting at the seams.

"Make way! Make way for Master Chaucer!" Harry bellowed in my ear, and he thrust me down between a skinny, suspicious-looking rogue and a boisterous, ample woman who clearly liked talking as much as she liked eating. Soon, there were huge dishes, piled high with food, arriving at each table. The ale was good and the wine was strong and both flowed freely, whetting everyone's appetites and loosening their tongues. We were a motley gathering of strangers, and I sat back and did what I loved best... observing other people.

The first of the pilgrims who caught my eye was a well-dressed nun – a **Prioress** in fact (high up in her convent) and known as Madam Eglantine. A most fastidious person.

"I can't bear to see any living thing in pain," she declared. "I weep if I see a mouse caught in a trap." She also had a little dog (against Church rules) which she fed with choice morsels from the table. "Only the best for *ma cherie*," she said.

She was very proud of her French (though by her accent I'm not sure she'd ever been to France). And never have I seen such table manners! Not one crumb fell from her tender lips, nor did any sauce drip onto her breast. "This is how they eat at court," she informed us all, daintily adjusting her veil to reveal more of her pretty face. She had with her a **Priest** called John – a handsome fellow with charming manners. The Prioress seemed rather put out when he talked to the other pilgrims.

Then there was a **Miller** – Robin by name, but I had to look twice to check this was a man and not a beast. Big and burly, barrel-chested: "I can heave a door off its hinges," he boasted, "or break it with my head."
He had a red beard as broad as a spade, a mouth as big as a furnace and wide black nostrils the size of chimneys. But his crowning glory had to be the wart on the tip of his nose. There was a tuft of hairs on it, as red as the bristles in a sow's ears. He spent the evening telling scurrilous stories (funnily enough, the Prioress did not approve) and boasting about his skill at stealing wheat from his customers.

A thin man, sitting quietly in the corner, was a **Clerk** from Oxford, a scholar studying Logic – that was just about all I could glean from him. He was so silent, I found myself forgetting he was there.
He picked at his food with bony fingers, and by his threadbare clothes I guessed all his meagre earnings went to feed his love of learning. He didn't seem to notice what went on around him. When he went to bed, I'm sure it was to dream of great philosophers, and libraries full of precious books.

Near to the Clerk, but ignoring him completely, sat

# The Prologue

a **Monk**. Not for this man the life a monk ought to live, shut away from the world in prayer and study. "I don't give a plucked hen for that," he said to anyone who would listen, his eyes twinkling merrily.

He loved nothing more than to go out hunting on one of his fine horses, and to eat and be merry, putting delicious roasted swan into his round fat belly. The sleeves of his monk's habit, I saw, were edged with squirrel-fur (the finest in the land) and on his feet were boots of soft, supple leather.

A little way off sat a **Manciple**. He seemed a thrifty fellow. His job was to buy provisions for lawyers up in London. "I'm not a learned man," he said, with a chuckle, "but I can still hoodwink all those lawyers. They think they're so clever, managing rich men's lands, but I've got them wrapped around my finger. I just say I spend more than I do, and keep the profits," he told us, patting his jangling pockets.

The Clerk  The Nun's Priest  The Prioress  The Monk  The Manciple  The Miller

Right next to me – I couldn't ignore her any longer – sat a lady spilling over the bench with her ample hips and flamboyant clothes. I swear, her headscarf alone must have weighed ten pounds. The **Wife of Bath** she called herself, and she kept roaring with laughter at her own jokes.

"I'm always going on pilgrimages," she told me. "I've picked up a husband that way before now," she added in what was meant to be a whisper, but nearly deafened me. "Though I've had more men than that," she chortled, winking at me. In the town of Bath she's well known as a cloth maker – a fine businesswoman, I believe, though equally skilled in the game of love, it seems.

Then there was a **Friar**, whose job it was to beg and preach for a living, listening to people's confessions and then forgiving them their sins. He'd forgive them easily enough – though only if he was sure of getting a gift in

The Franklin   The Reeve   The Wife of Bath   Chaucer   The Friar

return. I never met a man with such a silver tongue. He could talk an old woman out of her last penny, he was so well-practised at preaching in his lisping voice. He knew every tavern in every town and was on the best terms with the barmaids. Of course, he avoided beggars and lepers – they were far beneath him.

Wedged in opposite the Wife of Bath sat a **Reeve** – Oswald was his name. A carpenter by trade, as well as land-manager for a wealthy lord. "No one can pull the wool over my eyes," he rasped. "I know every trick in the book." As he sat there, fingering his rusty sword, I got the impression he wasn't averse to using tricks himself.

He kept apart from us all, his narrow eyes flicking from side to side, as if we might pick his pockets at any moment. "My lord's tenants are more afraid of me than of the plague," he boasted at one point – and I found it easy to believe him. He didn't join in the general merriment, but after eyeing up the barmaids, slunk off alone to bed on his long, stick-like legs.

Then there was the **Franklin**. It would be hard to find a man in England so fond of good food and fine wine. He liked a drop or two in the morning but, best of all, he loved to give lavish dinners. "It snows food and drink in my house!" he said, throwing open his arms with a joyous smile on his merry face (although if the food wasn't perfect, then the cook was for it).

He was a landowner, a Member of Parliament and a Magistrate, but I could tell by the glint in his eye that this gentleman lived for fun and pleasure.

You wouldn't want to make an enemy of *him* I thought, as I noticed the Shipman. A dagger hung from his neck and he was tanned brown as a nut, a real rough diamond.

He was a ship's captain and often made the trip to France, bringing back wine (and drinking his fair share of it in the night watches, when the wine merchants were asleep below deck). He'd sailed the world, and his beard had been blown about by many a storm. A great navigator and a brilliant seaman – a vicious fighter too, when the need arose – and he could even ride a horse (well, in a fashion).

Next to him – what a contrast – sat a Doctor. He wore a blue and scarlet coat, lined with the finest silk. He must have earned a lot of money. "But I don't spend it, I save it all up," he said. I've heard that gold is the best medicine – well, gold is what the good doctor loved best of all.

Nowhere in the world could you find a man who knew as much about surgery or medicine. He was an expert at astrology too, and whenever he had a patient, he'd make them wait until exactly the right hour to give his treatment (according to the stars). He had remedies and charms, talismans and all sorts of cures. Whatever you had wrong with you, he had something for it.

There was also a Parson, a good man, a parish priest. He was wise, kind and always patient when times were hard. And they often were. His parish was miles wide, but if anyone needed help he'd walk through rain and wind to visit them, no matter who they were.

He wasn't one to go waltzing off to London to hobnob with the Archbishop – he was a good shepherd who looked after his flock. He taught by example and never looked down on sinners. You couldn't find a better priest, I swear.

A **Cook** sat next to the Parson, gulping down huge mouthfuls of London ale. His name was Roger – I'd met him before. He could boil, roast and fry with the best of them. Shame about that huge weeping ulcer on his leg – not exactly appetizing!

There was a **Merchant**, too, with a forked beard, a fashionable outfit and boots with great big fancy clasps. He moaned a lot about his wife (he claimed she was a match for the devil, and his face looked so glum I believed it to be true). He also boasted about all the profits he'd made, though later I heard he was actually in debt. Funny, but I never learned his name...

The Shipman   The Doctor   The Merchant   The Parson   The Cook

There was a **Knight**, too. Hot-foot from waging war, in a tunic marked with rusty stains from his chain mail, the knight was here to give thanks for his safe return. He had fought all his life, he said, in faraway lands, both for his faith and his King. He'd taken part in fifteen famous battles and was three times picked to fight a mortal combat: he always killed his man. But for all his fame, he was wise, modest and mild-mannered as a maid. Above all else, he loved truth, honour and freedom. He was the very image of a noble knight.

With the Knight came his son, the **Squire**. He was as lively and fresh as his father was serious and grave. His hair was so wavy, it looked as if he'd curled it, and he was wonderfully strong and athletic. He couldn't have been more than twenty, but he'd already fought, with credit, in battle. His most ardent wish, though, was to

The Squire  The Summoner  The Knight  The Pardoner  Harry Bailey

impress his lady-love. He could sing, ride, dance, joust, draw and play the flute. "But all that counts for nothing unless I can win my love!" he sighed. And it was this thought that kept him up each night.

Past the Squire I spotted a fiery-red face in the gloom. Peering closer, I saw it was covered in large pustules and boils. That was the **Summoner**. The Prioress had been sitting near him, "But I couldn't stand it," she said. "He reeks of garlic and leeks."
He downed his wine so quickly it kept dribbling into his mangy beard. "I can speak Latin," he slurred at me, "*questio quid juris*?" I replied in Latin, but it turned out he only knew the one phrase (and he said it over and over again). His job was to summon wrongdoers to the Church courts. But he was such a generous fellow, that for money or wine he'd let anyone go.

With him was a **Pardoner**. Not a pretty sight: thin, yellow hair spread over his shoulders, each sparse strand clinging to his scalp like a rat's tail. But he liked to show off these lank clumps, so he didn't wear a hood. His eyes were as big and bulging as a hare's and it was hard to tell his voice from a bleating goat's. Even so, he was very successful at his job, which was selling holy pardons and relics, hot from Rome. He had a piece of the Virgin Mary's veil (which looked suspiciously like a pillowcase) and a bottle full of saints' bones (they were really pigs').
With his double-talk, he tricked as many people as he could into buying his wares, and he made a packet –

more in a day than a parson could in a month or two.

By the time I'd gone through them all, I was feeling very sleepy. The room was hot and stuffy, the talk loud and raucous. I stumbled off to find my bed, thinking that, with luck, one or two of this strange gathering might give me an idea for a story...

I woke early the next morning, and met all the pilgrims stumbling sleepily into the yard in front of the inn.

"Ah! Ladies and gentlemen," Harry greeted us all. "Aren't you all glad that we decided last night to make the pilgrimage together. A brilliant idea of mine!"

I looked around in some surprise, but everyone was nodding.

"And I've had an even better idea," he went on. "Let's each tell a story on our way. Whoever tells the most amusing or instructive tale, will have his supper paid for by us all on our return, at this very inn." Clever Harry, I thought. A brilliant money-making scheme for him!

The Reeve was about to make an objection, but even as he opened his mouth, Harry went on, "And anyone who questions what I say, will pay all our expenses on the way!"

The Reeve quickly shut his mouth again.

"Are we all agreed?" asked Harry.

"Yes, indeed," we said, hastily.

"And you'll be our judge?" I asked.

"Ah! Geoffrey," boomed Harry. "How kind of you to ask."

As soon as we were mounted on our horses and ready

to go, Harry produced a bunch of straw, clutched in his huge fist. "We'll draw lots to see who should tell the first tale."

"Ladies first!" butted in the Wife of Bath. "Shouldn't I begin?"

But our host was already gathering the pilgrims around him so each could pick a straw, calling back the Clerk whose horse had wandered off, and beckoning to the Prioress, who was trying to keep her distance from the Summoner, I think.

We looked at our straws and it was the Knight who'd drawn the shortest one.

# The Knight's Tale
(about Palamon and Arcite who both loved Emily)

"Very right and proper that such a noble person should begin," simpered the Prioress. All the other pilgrims were relieved too – no one had wanted to be first. The Knight, well-bred as he was, knew there was no way out – he must play by the rules of the game.

"Well, I'll make a start!" he said with a willing smile. "Hear my tale, then. Listen as we go."

And with that we set off, and he began...

Trumpets blew. Dogs barked. Hooves pounded over the dusty ground as Duke Theseus returned home to Athens. "Make way for the victorious conqueror," called the herald, "and for his new wife, Hippolyta, Queen of the Amazons!"

Crowds lined the sides of the road, cheering and craning their necks to see the new Queen. They had all heard of the Amazons – a fierce tribe of women warriors, recently vanquished by Athenian men. At Hippolyta's side rode her sister, Emily, more beautiful than all the flowers in the month of May.

# The Knight's Tale

Duke Theseus was filled with pride as he showed off his new bride, but as he neared the city gates, his ears were pierced by a pitiful wailing. A group of women, dressed in black, threw themselves in his path.

"Help us!" cried the eldest woman, falling at Duke Theseus's feet. "We are sorrowing widows – our husbands died attacking the evil King Creon of Thebes. Even now their bodies lie piled outside in a rotting heap, left out for the dogs to eat. Creon will not let us bury our dead."

"By my honour as a knight," Duke Theseus declared, "I'll have my revenge on this tyrant, Creon." Not stopping for a moment, he sent Hippolyta and Emily on to Athens, and with his men, marched straight to Thebes.

He chose his battlefield and left it soaked in blood. King Creon was among the dead, killed in a fair fight. That night, Theseus rested, while his men scoured the field, picking over the dead bodies for swords and shields. There they found two knights, lying side by side, both bleeding but living still. By their coats of arms they saw they were royal cousins, Palamon and Arcite. Carefully, they carried them back to Theseus's tent.

"Send them to Athens," Theseus ordered, "and lock them in our strongest tower. That's where they'll end their days."

When Palamon and Arcite woke, they found themselves in a small round room with thick stone walls and one barred window, which let in the barest chink of light. Their wounds recovered, but their hearts were sore.

"At least we are together, cousin," said Palamon.

Arcite gripped his hand eagerly. "Together, as we always swore."

The months passed, through a cold winter into a glorious spring. Palamon paced the upper rooms, hearing in his echoing footsteps the sound of his future, trapped within the tower. With a sigh, he turned to the window and gazed out on the palace gardens below. At that moment, Emily wandered into view amidst the greenery, singing like an angel as she plucked flowers for her hair.

Palamon let out a cry and started back, as if he had been struck.

"Cousin! What is it?" called Arcite, running to his side. "Are you ill?"

"I have been pierced through my eye, right to the heart. The wound is killing me. There's a lady in the garden, so beautiful I don't know if she's a woman or a

goddess. I think she must be Venus, Goddess of Love." So saying, he fell to his knees and prayed to Venus to free them both.

As Palamon prayed, Arcite ran to the window and feasted his eyes on Emily. Her beauty struck him too, and like his cousin he fell back, crying, "I must win her! I'd rather die than lose her!"

"What are saying, cousin?" said Palamon, rounding on him. "Are you joking?"

"No, I swear."

"You traitor! How dare you love the same lady as I? We promised never to betray each other, but to be like brothers till we died. I loved her first. You must help me in my quest."

"I loved her first," snapped Arcite, "as a woman! You thought she was a goddess. Mine is the real love – the love of a human being. And even if you did see her first, haven't you heard the phrase, *all's fair in love and war?*"

On and on they fought, like two dogs over a bone, even though they had no hope of ever escaping their prison home...

Until, one day, Duke Theseus's great friend, Perotheus, came to stay. He'd known and loved Arcite, and begged Theseus to let him go.

"Only on certain terms," Theseus decided at last. "He can go free, but must never return to Athens. If I ever find him on my land again, I'll sever his head with my own sword."

When he heard the news, Arcite wept. "I'll be in a worse prison than before. At least if I stay in the tower I can gaze on Emily. Palamon, your prison is like a paradise compared to mine! You are near her, and by some chance, may win her. I shall be in exile and despair."

After Arcite had left, Palamon cried for days. His mind festered on the thought that somehow his traitor cousin would return to Athens and gain Emily's love "...and all while I lie dying in a cage!" he moaned.

"Who is worse off?" the Knight wondered aloud. "The imprisoned Palamon, who can gaze upon his love? Or Arcite, free to come and go, but banned from seeing Emily again?"

In reply, the Miller snored. He'd been drinking ever since daybreak and had nodded off on his plodding horse.

"Palamon's worse off!" declared the Friar. "At least Arcite can find another woman. He's young, after all," he added with a knowing chuckle.

The Squire frowned. "I hardly think that's the point," he said. "This is a story about true love."

"What about Emily?" asked the Wife of Bath, so loudly that the Miller woke with a start. "Has anyone asked what she wants?"

The Knight coughed. "Yes, well," he said, "an interesting question. Now, on with my tale..."

Arcite reached Thebes, but he was sick with love. He couldn't eat or drink. His skin turned sallow, his eyes hollow, and he was soon a shrunken image of his former self. For a year, then two, his life dragged on, his mind oppressed with longing. Then, one night, he had a dream: the winged god, Mercury, appeared before him, saying, "To Athens you must go." With a start, Arcite woke and knew his dream spoke the truth. "I am so altered no one will know me," he told himself. "And, anyway, I must see Emily again, even if I die for it."

As soon as Arcite arrived in Athens, he offered his services at court, and got a lowly job, running errands for his true love. He called himself Philostrate, and for his kindness and his gentleness was loved by everyone at court. But still, he had to worship Emily from afar.

Meanwhile, buried away within his tower, Palamon wore himself away in grief. Seven years passed, until, at last, a friend came to his aid. He drugged the prison guards and, shortly after midnight, Palamon broke out. Under cover of darkness he fled the palace and its grounds, running as fast as he could to the woods. "I'll go to Thebes," he told himself. "I'll raise up an army and come back to win Emily. Tonight, though, I shall rest."

He lay down to sleep beneath a thicket. As dawn broke, another man came wandering into the woods. He sighed as he walked, wishing a thousand things were other than they were... "If Thebes were not at war with Athens, if I were not a slave serving my enemy but a duke again, known by my own name, if Emily would but look at me..."

Palamon, with a pale face and wild hair, sprang like a madman from the thicket, shouting, "Arcite! You foul, wicked traitor! My cousin, sworn to love me, you've lied about your name and loved my lady, you'll die for this..."

He ran at him, sword raised. Arcite was ready for him, and in that quiet grove, steel clashed with steel.

"Love is free, you fool!" Arcite spat at him.

Their swords slashed through the morning air and clashed again, glinting in the sunlight. Arcite, cruel as a tiger, and Palamon raging like a lion... they were two circling animals, spattered with each other's blood.

They fought so hard, they never heard the sound of hooves on the forest floor. Duke Theseus, out to hunt a stag, followed by Queen Hippolyta and Emily, came galloping into the glade.

In one bound, Theseus leaped between the fighting pair, crying, "Stop! Put up your swords. Who are you both, that you dare fight upon my land?"

"My lord," announced Palamon. "I may as well confess, since both of us here will go happily to our deaths. This is Arcite, your deadly enemy, banished from Athens. He has made a fool of you these seven years by playing the part of Philostrate. And I am Palamon, no less, escaped from your prison. We burn with love for Emily and for her we are prepared to die."

"I have your confession from your own lips," said Theseus. "As you suggest, you shall die for this."

"No!" wept Emily and the Queen, falling on their knees. "Have mercy, Theseus," they cried, moved both by the sight of blood and this tale of true love.

Theseus paused, and his anger passed. He looked deep into his noble heart and remembered that he, too, had once been stung by the arrows of love. "The Goddess of Love can make what she likes of the human heart," he thought. "These two think they act with sense, but they are slaves to love." Aloud, he said, "Look at you both! You have given up your chance of freedom, all for a woman who doesn't even know you exist. I have decided to forgive you... but Emily cannot marry you both."

Palamon and Arcite, now on their knees, awaited Theseus's judgement like lambs.

"You must leave here for a year," said Theseus. "But, after the twelve months are up, return to me, each with a hundred knights. I will hold a great tournament, and the winner gains fair Emily's hand."

At this Palamon and Arcite sprang up, filled with joy. They thanked Duke Theseus and set out for Thebes, promising to return... and fight another day.

"And now," said the Knight, turning round to make sure that all the pilgrims were listening still, "let me tell you about the stadium Duke Theseus built for the tournament..."

I have to confess that, at this point, even I thought I might nod off. I was enjoying this tale of courtly love, but did I really want to know about the tiered seating, the carvings, sculptures, paintings on the walls? Our noble Knight did seem to be going on a bit.

We heard every detail of the furnishings, including the temples Theseus built – one for Mars, the God of War, one for Venus, Goddess of Love, and another for Diana, Goddess of Maidens and the Hunt...

"And what happened to Palamon and Arcite?" I asked, to jog him on. It seemed to do the trick.

"Yes, I won't linger on the details," said the Knight, obviously unaware that was what he'd just done. "I'll move quickly back to Arcite and Palamon..."

They returned a year to the day. Each came with a hundred of the finest knights, dressed in shining battle gear. Some carried swords, others wielded steel maces and battle axes – one even rode a golden chariot pulled by huge white bulls. It was an amazing sight. On the morning of the fight, Palamon woke with the lark, and made his way to the temple of Venus – for he chose to worship the Goddess of Love.

"Take pity on me," he prayed. "I don't ask for honour and glory in battle. All I desire is for you to give me Emily, so she's mine and mine alone. But if you decide Arcite should have her for a wife, then let me die tomorrow on the end of Arcite's spear."

After he spoke, the statue of Venus began to shake. "It's a sign!" cried Palamon. "She's heard my prayers."

Emily, too, was up with the sun. But she chose to say her prayers in Diana's temple.

"Oh, fair Goddess of the woods and glades," she prayed. "You know I'd rather roam free forever than be a wife or be with child. If you can, set peace between Arcite and Palamon."

All at once, the fires burning at the altar flickered and went out. Diana, dressed as a huntress with bow in hand, appeared before Emily.

"It has already been decided," she said, "that you must marry one of them. But which it will be I cannot tell…" Before Emily could ask her more, Diana vanished as quickly as she'd come. Emily bowed her head and turned for home. "If I must have one," she thought, "then let it be the one who desires me most."

An hour later, Arcite knelt before Mars – God of War. In his grim, dark temple, he gave a sacrifice and said his prayers. "I am more racked and torn with love than any living creature ever was. Bring me victory tomorrow – that's the only hope I shall ever have of winning Emily."

On his last word, the temple doors began to rattle and the ground to quake. Trembling, Arcite stumbled back. A single word echoed around the temple walls: "Victory!" it seemed to say. Daring to hope, Arcite rushed to prepare for battle. Immediately, a furious row broke out between the gods. It was Mars against Venus,

each determined that their man should win.

Their arguments raged across the skies, until, at last, old Saturn stepped in. "I'll see that your knight, Palamon, wins his lady," he promised Venus. "Mars will help his man, but you can trust me. You'll see..."

Back on earth, crowds flocked to Duke Theseus's palace, to see the great tournament take place. Bets were laid on all the different knights. "I'll back Blackbeard!" shouted one man, while another chose Baldhead.

"See how grim he looks! And that sword must be twenty pounds in weight. He'll put up a good fight."

Duke Theseus rose like a god from his golden throne and everyone fell silent. "This is not, after all, a fight to the death," he declared. "Each knight only has one strike and any man pulled to the stakes at the sides may not enter the fray again. Now – let the fight begin..."

Trumpets blared. Fanfares trilled. Palamon entered through the East Gate, his white banner fluttering in the breeze. Arcite came marching from the west, red banner blazing.

The knights dug in their spurs, made ready with their spears, while swords flashed silver in the sun.

Some brought down their maces, crushing bone. Others came crashing down beneath their horses, to lie on the blood-soaked ground. And in the heaving throng, Arcite sought out Palamon.

Filled with jealous hatred, both thirsted to hurt the other. They rained down blows until their blood came gushing out. Palamon raised his spear, aiming to bite the shaft deep into Arcite's flesh. But with a fierce blow to the chest, Palamon was tossed to the stakes.

More than anything, he longed to go and fight again, but by Duke Theseus's rules the battle was over. Arcite had won.

The crowd cheered. Palamon, like Venus in the heavens, wept bitter tears. Old Saturn looked on. "Stop your tears, Venus," he said. "Mars's man may have won, but you'll have your victory still."

Arcite heard the cheers; he took off his helmet, so he could gaze at the prize he'd won... Emily, after all these years. He spurred on his horse and set off across the battlefield, his eyes fixed on Emily's smiling face. And it was at that moment, of Arcite's greatest joy, that Saturn sent a thunderbolt from the sky. It struck the ground with a sudden, sickening blast.

Arcite, unprepared, was flung from his terrified, bucking horse, high into the air. The world whirled around him. He was free as air. For a moment he hung, suspended, then landed heavily, head-first, like one already dead.

Everyone came running, hovering over Arcite's motionless body. "Take him to the palace," ordered Duke Theseus. "Lay him on my bed."

Emily and Palamon rushed to his side, Emily weeping all the while. She watched the colour drain from Arcite's face, and even as Arcite forced open his bloodshot eyes, he felt the first flutterings of death.

"Emily," he rasped, "queen of my heart – and my sweetest enemy, for you I go alone now to my grave. And Palamon, my dearest cousin – how I've hated you. Now, as I face death, may I speak as a true knight should, with wisdom, chivalry and humility, and ask that Emily marries you, in my place. No man is worthier to be loved. Emily... I know he will serve you all your life."

Then death, with its chill grasp, stole into his heart. Arcite spoke his last words: "Hold me, Emily!" and died.

Tears flowed through Athens as the news spread. Duke Theseus poured his grief into the funeral pyre, making it as high as heaven with flames that licked the stars.

The crowds watched Arcite's body being placed upon the fire. As his body burned, his ashes floated on the air, then fluttered, moth-like, to the muddy ground.

After the funeral was over, Duke Theseus took Emily and Palamon by the hand.

"Out of great sadness, let us bring true happiness," he declared.

"Take pity on noble Palamon, Emily, and have him for a husband; so that from two sorrows, we'll have one perfect joy."

"Now, that's my tale told," declared the Knight. "And God bless you all."

"And so they lived happily ever after?" sneered the Merchant.

"Indeed," replied the Knight. "Palamon lived the rest of his days in bliss, loving Emily and equally beloved by her. Never a cross word was spoken between them."

"A likely story..." the Merchant muttered beneath his breath.

But the Prioress was shedding tears. "So sad," she sniffed. "Poor Arcite... that chivalrous flower! His love came to nothing. Oh! It is almost too much for me... see how delicate and sensitive I am!"

"But all human life must come to an end," the Knight said, comfortingly. "After all, we are but pilgrims here on earth, journeying between this life and the next. And remember, Arcite had an honourable death. What more could any good man want?"

"Quite a lot more," said the Friar, casting a leer at the Wife of Bath.

"A very noble tale!" interrupted Harry, our host. "A fine beginning to our contest, thank you, sir," he said to the Knight.

# The Miller's Tale

(about John the Carpenter and
the End of the World)

"The question is," said Harry, "who thinks they can do better than the Knight?"

"I have a tale!" the Miller shouted. "By blood and bones, it's far, far better than the Knight's tale, if I say so myself."

The Miller was as white as a sheet, and appeared to have lost his hat. He was slurring his words, and lurching from side to side in his saddle like a ship in stormy seas.

"Perhaps another time," said Harry.

"No! Now!" said the Miller. "I will not be silenced! Either I tell my brilliant tale, or I shall ride on alone."

For myself, I didn't think that would be too tragic an outcome, but Harry backed down.

"Alright, good luck to you. Let's see if you can string a sentence together."

"Before we start," the Miller said, punctuating his speech with loud and persistent hiccups, "I admit I am not exactly – *hic* – at my absolute best this morning, and I – *hic* – apologize if I muddle my words a little, but here goes..."

# The Miller's Tale

he sun was singing and the birds were shining, and a stupid old carpenter was sitting with his pretty young wife, and he was about to be made a terrible fool of...

"Stop!" shouted Oswald the Reeve. "Is this a tale about adultery?"

"You're very quick," said the Miller. "Married, I take it?"

"What do you mean by that?" bawled Oswald.

"As everyone knows," the Miller said, "the man who hasn't been fooled by his wife is a bachelor. But, I'm sure your wife is very well behaved, Oswald."

The Miller belched, wiped his mouth, and continued: "I expect she's positively dripping with innocence. For myself, I feel that we shouldn't try to delve too deeply into the two great mysteries of life: the wonders of the cosmos... and women."

The Miller sighed.

"Don't ever ask your wife what she does when you're not there," he shouted, pointing a swaying arm at each pilgrim in turn (including, curiously enough, the Prioress).

"And, I warn you, don't ever even try to understand what she's thinking. You'll only be horribly, horribly frightened."

With that, the Miller began his vulgar tale in his own, crude language, swearing, flailing in his saddle and pausing every now and then to take a long swallow of ale. It wasn't what you might call a noble story.

Indeed, if it wasn't that I'd decided to record all the tales, I would never have included it. So if you'd prefer a virtuous tale, complete with shining knights, fiery dragons and innocent maidens, please skip on to another story.

For you'll find nothing more noble in the Miller's tale than foolishness and farting...

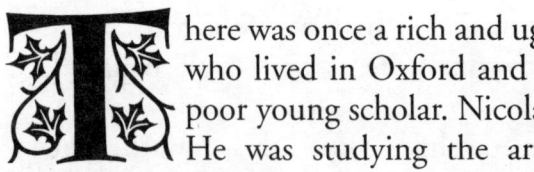

There was once a rich and ugly old carpenter who lived in Oxford and kept a lodger, a poor young scholar. Nicolas was his name. He was studying the arts, but his real passion was astrology.

"Nicolas," a friend would say, "what day should I take my pig to market?" And Nicolas would look into his books and make his calculations.

"You must go on Friday," he'd reply. "For on Friday Venus shall be conjoined with Mars, and Mercury is on the wane. Also, that's the only day the market's open. Cheddar and Franciscans will also be lucky for you this week."

Nicolas built up quite a reputation with his fortune telling. And although he looked as innocent as a little girl, he had a wicked way with the ladies. So he spent his time studying the stars, meeting women and spending his friends' money. It was altogether a very pleasant life.

# THE MILLER'S TALE

The ugly old carpenter, whose name was John, had a wife called Alison, who was much younger than he was. She was an absolute knockout. She was eighteen years old, and she spent her days running around like a frisky young colt.

John didn't trust her one bit, for she was so young and pretty and, as he admitted himself, he had a face like a horse's backside. He was quite right to be wary. For one day, while John was out, Nicolas went straight up to Alison and announced:

"If you don't come to bed with me right now, I'll die."

Still, Alison wasn't having any of it. She ran to the other end of the room and shrieked:

"If you come one step closer, I'll scream so loud half the street will be here in a second!"

"Alison," Nicolas said, "don't break my heart. You could make me so happy, my darling." He batted his eyelashes at her. "And no one has to know a thing."

"Don't even think about it," said Alison. And that was that. But whenever the carpenter went out, Nicolas always appeared out of nowhere like a little lost schoolboy.

"Please, Alison, please say yes."

He pestered and pestered her until finally, one day, she crumbled.

"Fine," she said, "I'll give you a kiss, and maybe a little more. But, if my husband suspects a thing, it'll be the end of both of us."

"Don't worry your pretty little head about that," Nicolas replied. "I wouldn't be much of a scholar if I didn't know how to get the better of a carpenter."

And he walked away, whistling a merry tune.

The next Sunday Alison went to church, as she was a very devout young lady. There she saw a young man called Absolon. She could hardly miss him – he had an enormous mop of curly blond hair and a small, weaselly face. His skinny legs were wrapped in tight scarlet stockings and he wore a billowing white cassock, which came down to his knobbly knees. He had what might be called a unique style. When Alison walked into the church, Absolon fell in love with her at first sight.

Among his many talents, Absolon was an expert dancer and his speciality was the Oxford Whirl. This involved flinging his legs in all conceivable directions and praying that no one got seriously hurt.

That very night, he took his tambourine and whirled and whirled until he ended up under Alison's window.

"Oh lady mine," he sang in a high falsetto. "My one and only love!"

Inside the house, John woke up and nudged Alison.

# THE MILLER'S TALE

"Is that Absolon yodelling under the window?" he asked Alison.

"Well, yes, it is, actually," said Alison apologetically.

"Can't you tell him to go away?"

"Go away!" Alison shouted. But Absolon kept singing all night, and the next night, and the night after that…

"Is this what hell sounds like?" shouted John, on the eleventh night. "Can we please drop a rock on his head and put a stop to this?"

Down below, Absolon was starting to get desperate.

"Alison," he shouted, "I'll give you anything – if you'll only open your window and give me one kiss. Would you like some honey? Some socks? Marzipan? A thimble? I've got some lovely ale down here. It's very good."

But Alison's window remained firmly closed.

"Fine," Absolon shouted, "how much do you want? I've got ten silver pieces. Alright, let's say fifteen. Thirty? Fifty. A hundred. A hundred silver pieces for one kiss!"

There was no reply, but Absolon still did not give up. He went to act in a local play and landed the part of The Tyrannical and Murderous Villain: King Herod. Against all his expectations, the sight of him ordering the slaughter of thousands of innocent children did not make Alison fall instantly in love with him.

Alison had nothing against men with knobbly knees, scarlet stockings, curiously high voices and negligible acting talent. But she was already deeply in love – with her young, sly lodger, Nicolas. She couldn't get him out of her head. She just had to get her husband out of the way.

One day, when John was out, Alison and Nicolas came up with a plan. If it succeeded, Alison would be able to spend the night with Nicolas.

"We're all set," said Nicolas, clapping his hands. "If your husband asks where I am, say you haven't seen me, but you think I might be ill." With that, he slipped up to his room with a basket of food and shut his door.

Three days later, John was starting to wonder what had happened to his lodger. "I haven't heard a squeak out of Nicolas for days," he said to his servant, Robin. "He might be dead for all I know. Go and bang on his door, and see if you can get an answer."

So Robin ran up the stairs and hammered like mad on the door.

"Nicolas! Master Nicolas! Are you asleep?"

At the bottom of the door was a hole that the cat used to creep through. Robin crouched down, peeked through it, and there was Nicolas, sitting bolt upright on his bed, his eyes as wide as saucers.

Robin clattered back down the stairs. "He's in there alright – but I think he's in some sort of trance!"

"Help us, St. Frideswide!" John cried. "The dark powers of astrology have destroyed him!"

John started to pace around the room. "I always said that astrology was dangerous – and now this! D'you remember that fellow – what was his name?"

"George, was it?"

"Yes, that's it, he studied the stars. He went out one night, walked across a field, all the time staring up at the sky, and what do you think happened?"

"What?"

# THE MILLER'S TALE

"He fell headfirst into a claypit. That's what astrology can do to you. It's evil, Robin, and it must be stopped. Fetch me my staff. We must go and save his soul."

So John and Robin ran to Nicolas's room, threw themselves at his door, once, twice – and the third time they burst through it. There was Nicolas, sitting as still as a sphinx.

"Nicolas!" John shouted into his ear. "Come back to us, for God's sake! Wake up! Wake up!" John shook him and shook him until he wobbled like jelly, but Nicolas didn't say a word. He just stared ahead vacantly.

"He's possessed by evil spirits," said John. "We need a spell to banish them." He grabbed a crucifix from the wall and bellowed:

"Let the sign of the cross defend you from elfs, pixies, hobgoblins, tiny fairies, small fairies, medium-sized fairies, large fairies, left-handed fairies, right-handed fairies – and all other evil spirits of the night! We must protect the whole house from these tiny creatures of darkness," he added ominously, and he dashed around his house, sprinkling holy charms everywhere. He put them on the windowsill, in the milk jug, under his bed, and he hung two from his ears for good luck. Then he ran back to Nicolas's room and stared into his eyes.

Finally, Nicolas let out a great sigh. "Alas, why must the world end so soon?" he said.

"What do you mean?" said John.

"Get me a drink," Nicolas replied, with a sad, soulful look in his eyes. "Then I will tell you a terrible secret, a secret that will change your life forever."

John ran downstairs and was back in a moment with a jug of ale. When they'd both drunk as much as they wanted, Nicolas sprang up and bolted the door.

"John, my host and my dearest friend, I'm going to tell you a secret. You must promise not to tell a soul about it."

"I promise," said John.

"If you betray me, you'll turn quite mad."

"I won't."

"Alright," said Nicolas, "this is God's honest truth. The world is about to end."

"What?" John's eyes goggled.

"By gazing at the moon, I found out that next Monday night it will start to rain, and in less than an hour, the whole world will be flooded!"

"But my poor wife!" John cried, turning as white as a sheet, "my darling Alison! Is there nothing we can do?"

"Well yes, of course," answered Nicolas, drily. "You

must listen to the expert, which just so happens to be me. I may be able to save all three of us," he said casually. "Do you remember the tale of Noah and the ark?"

John nodded.

"And the trouble Noah had with all those animals? I bet he wished he'd just taken a rowing boat and a couple of his less annoying children. What was he thinking, setting out to sea with a bunch of potentially lethal animals? He got it all wrong. So, you see what you have to do."

John sat in silence for some moments. "Not really, no," he said.

"We need an ark," Nicolas said slowly, "but without the animals. We'll need a tub each – big enough for us to stretch our legs in. Now, when you've got the tubs, you'll have to hang them high up in the rafters, and build ladders so we can climb into them. We'll each need an axe, to cut the ropes when we're ready to float away. When the flood comes, the water will rise, and we'll all float out of the window and drift around for a day or two, just until the water goes down again. Got it?"

John nodded slowly.

"Oh, and bring some ale and some nice cheese. Just think of it as a lovely day out."

When John told Alison the news, he wanted to weep. He could almost see the raging torrents coming to destroy the world. But he pulled himself together and set to work. By Monday night, three tubs were hanging from the rafters, three wooden ladders led up to them, and John was exhausted. Nicolas, Alison and John all sat in their vats, waiting quietly for the appointed hour.

They waited and waited and soon enough, John fell asleep and began to snore. Nicolas and Alison tiptoed down their ladders and rushed to Alison's bedroom, where they spent a happy night together.

Later that night, Alison heard a familiar voice outside her window.

"Oh my lady love..."

"Oh go away, Absolon!" shouted Alison. "I've found someone else, and he's a lot better than you."

"But my darling," Absolon cried, "don't you love me at all?"

"I'm trying to sleep."

"Was ever true love so abused?" Absolon wailed.

"You'd better get away from that window, I tell you, unless you want your head to be abused by a large and pointy rock."

"Just one kiss! That's all I ask."

"Alright," she said. "If I kiss you, will you promise to go away?"

"I promise," said Absolon.

The night was pitch black and Absolon couldn't see a thing. As he stretched up to her window, Alison opened it and pushed Nicolas's face out into the darkness. Absolon reached up, took a deep breath, and kissed it.

"That's odd," he thought to himself. "Women don't usually have beards. But that was... definitely hairy."

The face disappeared, the window slammed shut and a torrent of giggles exploded from inside Alison's bedroom. "We really got him with that one," a man's voice said with a chuckle. Absolon's burning love turned

# The Miller's Tale

cold in an instant. He ran off down the road, weeping and cursing the whole of womankind. But in ten minutes he was back under Alison's window, with a red hot poker in his hand.

"My darling Alison," he called up. "My love! I've brought you a gold ring. It's yours for one more kiss."

Nicolas leaped out of bed again and flung open the window. This time he stuck his bare bottom right out into the air.

"Speak, my love!" said Absolon, "For I can't see where you are!"

Nicolas answered – by letting out a fart as loud as a thunderclap. The explosion left Absolon half blind. He coughed, choked and nearly fainted, but he had the poker in his hand, and he lunged boldly into the darkness.

"AYEEEEE!"

Nicolas's scream could be heard for miles around. He hopped madly around the room, clutching his behind.

"HELP! HELP! WATER!" he yelled.

"Water?" Inside his tub, John woke up with a start. "Water? Water! The flood!"

Straight away he cut his rope and down fell the tub with a tremendous clang.

"It's coming!" John shouted, "The flood is coming for us all!"

Soon, half the street had come running into the house to stare at the man lying in a tub, screaming his head off about the end of the world.

"It's terribly sad," Nicolas said, with one arm draped over Alison's shoulder, and another covering his tender backside. "The poor man seems to have completely lost his marbles."

And that is how the carpenter was made a fool of, and Absolon got an unusual kiss, and how sly Nicolas got what he wanted – and then couldn't sit down for a week.

Everyone had something to say about the Miller's tale. The Prioress, who might have shrieked, had covered her ears early on in the story. The Wife of Bath was grinning like a cat, the Friar chuckled, the Knight smiled, and even the Pardoner let out a snide laugh.

In fact, the only person who took exception to the Miller's tale was Oswald the Reeve, who just happened to be a carpenter.

# The Reeve's Tale

(about Surly Simpkin, Frightful Fanny
and Miserable Molly)

"Since the Miller told a tale about a carpenter, and I happen to be one, I've half a mind to pay him back with a tale about a miller," said Oswald. "And I'll keep the language crude and simple, just so the Miller understands it."

"It's only fair," said Harry. "Tit for tat."

"Fine!" said the Miller. "Say what you like. In fact, I could even help you, Oswald. I could teach you some long words, so you could make your tale more interesting."

"Cut it out," said Harry.

"Only trying to help," said the Miller.

"There's Greenwich on the right," Harry went on, "a den of villains, rascals and rapscallions if ever there was one."

As he said this, I wondered if Harry knew that I had recently moved to Greenwich. I was sure I'd already told him. However, I thought it probably wasn't the right time to mention this, especially in front of all the other pilgrims.

"So, come on," Harry went on, "let's not dawdle about. On with your tale, Oswald..."

At Trumpington, near Cambridge, there lived a miller. He was an excellent fisherman, a dab hand at the bagpipes and one of the slyest scoundrels in all England. He swindled as many of his customers as he could, as often as he could.

Every day the miller would swagger about the town in his bright red stockings with a long, curved dagger hanging from his waist. His wife would walk behind him, her chin held high in the air. She was very well educated, and consequently she never lowered herself to speak to any of the ordinary folk. If any man so much as dared to look at her, the miller would slice them from top to toe with his dagger – or at least that's what he said he'd do.

The miller's nickname was Surly Simpkin, and his wife's was Frightful Fanny. They had one daughter, Miserable Molly, who was as wide as she was tall. A large pug nose squatted on her otherwise uneventful face. She had forgettable brown eyes, unforgettably enormous thighs, and altogether she was a shocker – although she did have lovely hair, I'll say that for her.

Anyhow, the miller ground grain into flour for a certain college at Cambridge University, and it made the master of the college wild with rage to think how much flour the miller might be keeping back for himself. So, one day he sent for two young students, Alan and John – a fine pair of rascals – to help him.

"Take these two bags of grain to the miller," the master said. "And don't take your eyes off 'em for a second. I'm

# THE REEVE'S TALE

not having that swindler of a miller stealing any more of my flour."

So Alan and John rode straight to Simpkin's house, and knocked on the door.

"Simpkin!" said Alan. "How are you? And how's your beautiful wife and your simply ravishing daughter?"

"Not bad," said Surly Simpkin. "What brings you here?"

"We've got two sacks of grain for grinding," said John. "And you know, it's such a marvellous, mysterious thing, grinding grain, isn't it?"

Surly Simpkin looked dourly at John.

"I'd love to watch you work," John went on, "if it wouldn't be too much trouble?"

"No trouble at all," said Simpkin. And if you think I can't pull the wool over your eyes, you're even stupider than you look, he thought.

Surly Simpkin began to grind the grain. While the students were talking, he slipped into the yard where the students' horse stood. He untied its bridle, and the horse gave a loud whinny ("Aaeyyye!") and galloped away.

When all the grain had been ground into flour, John strolled into the yard.

"Alan," he shouted. "Where did you put the horse?"

"Outside," shouted Alan.

"It's gone."

"Gone?" said Alan.

"It's either gone... or it's invisible." They were both staring at the spot where the horse had been when the miller's wife appeared.

"Oh dear me," she said. "Has your horse run off? It's

51

probably miles away by now. You'd better hurry if you want to catch up with it before dark."

So Alan and John raced off after their horse, entirely forgetting their promise to keep watch on the flour.

After they'd gone, Simpkin hid two sacks of the students' flour, and took a great heap of it to his wife.

"Fanny, why don't you bake us something nice for dinner?" he said. And he settled down by the fire, while outside it started to pour with rain.

Miles away, Alan and John were sunk knee-deep in mud and misery. They had been chasing the horse for hours as it zigzagged wildly across the fields.

"This is impossible," said John. "We'll never catch it."

"There she goes!" Alan shouted, as he saw a speck moving far away.

They ran and ran after the horse, but every time they were close to it, it bolted. It was sometime after nightfall when the horse got stuck in a ditch, and Alan and John finally caught it.

"Perfect," said John, as they tramped back to the miller's house in the dark. "Our clothes are ruined."

# THE REEVE'S TALE

"I'm soaked to the skin."
"We look like right idiots."
"At least you didn't lose your shoes in the mud."
"Everyone's going to laugh at us..."
"...And Surly Simpkin will laugh most of all."

Simpkin was sitting snugly by his fire when he heard the students knocking on his door. They appeared to be dressed in mud from the neck down.

"Do you think we could have a bit of food, and a bed for the night? We're happy to pay for it," said John.

"Come on in," said Simpkin. "It's not a big house, but you'll squeeze in somewhere. No doubt with your great academic minds, you'll be able to do some kind of algebra, and turn my little house into a palace, eh?"

During dinner, Surly Simpkin drank steadily, while Frightful Fanny looked into the distance, and refused to speak to the common students, who had quite outstayed their welcome as far as she was concerned. Miserable Molly sat sadly between them, pushing her peas around and eating nothing. She looked as if she might burst into tears at any moment.

When they'd finished eating, Surly Simpkin hiccupped up the stairs to show the students their bed.

"As you can see, we're all in the one room. It's no castle, but it'll have to do," he said with a belch. "Me and Fanny will be in the big bed over there, that's Molly's bed in the corner, and you boys can share this bed here."

So they all got into their beds and, in a moment, Surly Simpkin fell asleep and began to snore. His snores got louder and louder and soon the walls were trembling.

"Can we re-name him Simpkin the Stupendous Snorer?" said John.

"I can't believe they sleep through this every night!" said Alan. As Alan and John clamped their hands to their ears, Frightful Fanny began snoring just as loudly as her husband. She took the soprano part to her husband's bass. Completing the musical trio was a virtuoso performance from Miserable Molly. As they all came to a magnificent crescendo, Alan sat up in bed.

"I can't take it any more," he said. "There's only one thing I can think of that will cheer me up. I'm going to kiss Miserable Molly."

"You WHAT?!" hissed John.

"I'm going to kiss Miserable Molly," he said. "If I have to put up with this all night, I want some kind of compensation."

"Don't do it!" said John. "Simpkin's got a dagger! You really don't want to make him angry."

Alan shrugged. "He doesn't scare me," he said, and began to creep towards the sleeping girl. John put his head in his hands as Molly blinked and woke up.

"Can I kiss you?" Alan whispered to her.

"Kiss me?" Molly considered the proposal for a moment, having never been asked for a kiss before. "Well... why?" she whispered.

"Why not?" whispered Alan.

"Well... go on then," Molly said quietly, "but be quick about it." And so Alan gave her a kiss, and Miserable Molly started to look a lot less miserable.

"You'd better get back to bed," she whispered. "If my dad wakes up, he'll kill you."

## THE REEVE'S TALE

Alan planted another kiss on her pug nose (which he'd begun to find rather adorable), and started to creep back to bed.

"Pssst – Alan," Molly hissed. "Before you go, take the flour my dad stole from you. It's hidden behind the back door."

Alan nodded and got back into bed with John.

"Guess what?" he said, giving John a sharp poke in the ribs. "I kissed her! I kissed Miserable Molly!"

"YOU WHAT?!!!"

Alan turned his head, and saw, to his horror, that he hadn't been talking to John at all. John was nowhere in sight, and Alan had got into bed with Surly Simpkin.

"You've been KISSING MY DAUGHTER?" Simpkin roared. He gave Alan a colossal punch on the nose. Alan fell back, lunged forward again, and belted Simpkin with a cracking punch to the jaw. Soon they were scrabbling about on the floor, whacking and biting and kicking each other as hard as they could.

In all the commotion, Frightful Fanny woke up.

"Oh me! Oh my!" she shrieked. "The students are having a brawl!" She grabbed a stick that was lying against the wall, saw something move in front of her, hit it with all her might – and struck her husband straight across the forehead.

The miller fell to the floor like a sack of flour.

"Oh goody," she said. "I've got one. How exciting!"

But the body on the floor groaned, and she heard a very familiar voice.

"Fanny," snarled Simpkin. "You utter nitwit... GET THOSE STUDENTS!"

But by now, Alan and John were nowhere to be seen. They had taken the flour and were riding to Cambridge as fast as their horse would carry them.

"Young men these days," sighed the Franklin. "I don't know. All these capers they get into! You can try and try, but some people just never learn..."

"Well, Oswald," said Harry. "You said you'd pay the Miller back, and you certainly did."

Oswald smiled grimly. "It's just a shame that the Miller himself wasn't with us to enjoy it."

I looked over at the Miller. He was slumped in his saddle, fast asleep, and coming from him were some of the most extraordinary snores that I have ever heard.

# The Man of Law's Tale

(about Constance and her Perilous Voyages)

Harry Bailey glanced up at the sky with a knowing eye, and pulled his horse around. "Pilgrims," he called, "it's not getting any earlier! This day's a quarter done already. Let's waste no more time. You're a Man of Law, aren't you?" he enquired, waving at the lawyer as he spoke. "You're bound by the same rules as all the rest. Tell us a tale, then, and I'll judge that you've kept to the letter of the law."

"Right you are," replied the lawyer. "I'm a man of my word. But I wouldn't want to bore you. I could have told you many a good old tale, but Master Chaucer here's been there before me – he's already done them all to death in his so-called poems."

At this point I became a little wary. I was hoping I'd pick up some new material on this journey, but some of the pilgrims seemed a little suspicious of telling their best tales in front of a writer. I decided I'd have to think of some way to throw them off the scent... Meanwhile, the Man of Law began.

"Settle down, there! Are you listening? I don't usually hold forth for free you know! Pray silence for my tale – you won't have heard this one before..."

he merchants in the marketplace quickly passed on the gossip. "Have you heard the news? The King's daughter, Princess Constance, is riding through town today – everyone will be there to watch."

Crowds thronged to see the procession, cheering and throwing flowers as Constance guided her white horse along the narrow streets. The princess smiled and waved, her long hair and scarlet cloak flowing behind her, and scattered gold coins for the poor as she went by.

"What beauty!"

"Yes – and what goodness!" agreed two merchants among the crowd. "She has fine looks without pride, youth without foolishness, and she is humble, courteous and charitable too. When we return to our own country, we must tell our Emperor about this princess. He loves to hear of marvels from distant lands."

The merchants hoisted sail that very day. Before

a month had passed, their ships brought them safely home, with their rich cargo of spices, satins and cloth of gold.

The Emperor was delighted with their news. "If all you say is true, then since the world began there was never anyone to match Princess Constance in goodness and beauty!" he exclaimed. "I must marry her! Already, I feel I can hardly live without her." And so he wrote to her father, the King, to ask for her hand in marriage.

When the King told Princess Constance the news, she turned pale. "My dear child," said the King. "Surely you won't turn this advantageous offer down? It is true that the Emperor lives far away, and we will be sad to see you go. But this marriage would make peace between our lands. It is your duty to think of your country before your own happiness."

Constance swallowed hard. "Father," she said, "I am still young and it is hard for me to leave you. This strange land is so distant, I fear I may never see you again. But I know it is my duty."

All too soon, the preparations were made and a ship was packed with wedding gifts. Constance said her tearful goodbyes, but waved and smiled bravely at the cheering crowd lining the dock. Before she knew it, the ship was hoisting sail and heading out to sea.

As Constance saw the land shrink to a faint line on the horizon, she knew there was only one thing to do. She turned and set her face firmly forward.

"It will all turn out for the best," she said.

But at the Emperor's palace, things were already moving against her. The Emperor had a mother, a wicked woman, in love with her power at court. She was as cunning as a snake, hiding her malice behind a smile. She imagined how it would be when her son married – Constance would take her place, steal her son's affections. So she gathered her lords around her to hatch a plan.

"My lords," she said, "You all know that my son is about to marry this foreigner, this princess from far away. I know my son – he is in love and, foolish boy, he will give the girl everything she wants. We will be cast aside – nothing will be the same again. But, my lords, I have a plan to make us safe for ever. Swear you will help me!" Every man there gave her his oath.

As the Emperor's mother smiled in satisfaction, Constance was nearing the end of her voyage. Crowds stood on the sandy shore, cheering and jostling to get a glimpse of the foreign princess. The Emperor himself was there to greet her. "Welcome!" he cried, kissing her cheek. "My bride to be! The reports were all true – such loveliness! I am truly the luckiest man alive."

The marriage was planned for the very next day. Constance hardly slept, and the wedding day went by in a whirl. Trumpets sounded, soldiers saluted and courtiers bowed and curtseyed. There was dancing, feasting and song. Amid the rejoicing, no one noticed a group of lords slowly gathering around the Emperor. But the Emperor's mother smiled. Her plan was working.

# The Man of Law's Tale

As she gave the signal, the lords threw back their cloaks and drew their daggers. The Emperor made no sound as they struck him; he fell forward, his blood staining the marble floor. Silence fell and the guests drew back in horror as the Emperor's mother stepped over the body of her dead son. "Learn from this, all of you," she snarled, "what happens if you cross me. I am your Empress now. Guards, seize that girl!"

They dragged Constance from the palace, still dressed in her wedding clothes. "Where are they taking me?" she wondered, but she didn't have long to wait. Sand dunes loomed into view and beyond them, the sea, stained red by the setting sun. All alone, at the edge of the water, stood a tiny boat.

"I'm to set you adrift." said a guard leading her up to the boat. "Poor girl, so young and pretty, and on your wedding day too. But I have my orders. There are no oars or sails – you'll just have to drift where the ocean takes you. But you'll find a basket in there with some food and water. I couldn't let you starve." And he pushed the boat out into the darkening water.

Once more, Constance watched while the land grew faint on the horizon, and she knew there was only one thing to do. She turned and set her face firmly forward. "It will all turn out for the best," she said.

For weeks the boat drifted, and Constance lost track of time. Her store of food and water grew smaller and smaller, and her fine wedding gown grew worn and tattered. But still she kept scanning the horizon, hoping to see land again soon.

One day, a faint smudge appeared in the distance. The boat drifted on and a craggy coast, guarded by sharp rocks, came into view. "If only the wind would blow the boat to shore!" wished Constance.

Suddenly, a wave caught the boat and swept it along, straight for the jagged rocks. With a grinding crunch, the boat splintered to pieces, casting Constance into the fierce waves. She struggled against the current until finally, somehow, she felt pebbles beneath her toes. With her last strength she crawled up the beach, overjoyed to feel solid land once more.

As she lay there, too tired to move or even speak, she felt someone bending over her. "She's alive!" cried a voice. "Stand back, give her some air!" She felt kind hands lifting her, carrying her up the beach. She opened her eyes. An old man smiled down at her. "Are you strong enough to walk a few steps? I live just over there." And Constance saw a huge castle towering over the cliffs. Leaning on the old man's arm, she limped up to the castle gate.

Soon, Constance was sitting before a blazing fire in the castle hall. The old man and his beaming wife wrapped Constance in blankets and fed her hot soup with a silver spoon.

"Now, my dear," said the old lady, taking her by the hand, "who are you and where do you come from? We can see that your clothes were once fine, though now they're ragged shreds. You must have been at sea for months, and in such a tiny boat! Tell us, what happened to you?"

Constance opened her mouth to reply, but somehow she just couldn't find the words. "Poor dear, it's the shock," said the old lady. "We won't ask you any more questions. You need food and sleep – and plenty of it!"

Days turned to weeks and weeks turned to months as the old couple nursed Constance back to health. As soon as she was better, Constance wanted to repay their kindness. She cooked and cleaned for them, and visited the village every day, caring for the poor and sick.

One day, a messenger rode up to the castle gate. "My Lord Allen is on his way," he cried. "He will be here by nightfall!"

The castle was suddenly bustling with servants scurrying to and fro, airing bedding, polishing windows and preparing food. Constance sought out the old couple, to ask what was happening.

"Lord Allen owns this castle," said the old man, shaking out a tapestry.

"Yes, we just run things for him while he's away," said the old lady, plumping up a cushion. "Now you're well again, you'll have to tell him how you came here."

Towards sundown, a grand procession came into view. Horses whinnied and jingled their bridles, knights brandished their weapons and heralds sounded their trumpets. At the head of them all rode a young and handsome man. A sword studded with jewels hung at his side and gold rings glittered on his fingers. Behind him rode a lady, richly dressed in fine satin, and with a haughty air. "That's Lord Allen and Lady Donegild, his mother," the old man told Constance.

The lord and lady dismounted and led the crowd into the castle hall. A great feast lay ready for them, and the eating and drinking, singing and laughing went on far into the night.

As the last weary guests went to find their beds, Lord Allen called the old man aside. "Tell me," he said, "who was that lady who sat by you at the feast? Surely I have not seen her here before – I would have remembered that beautiful face."

The old man told him of the shipwreck, and Lord Allen was intrigued by the tale. "A woman of mystery!" he smiled. "I will speak to her tomorrow." But Lord Allen's mother listened closely. "A likely story!" Donegild said sourly to herself. "She may have convinced those two old fools, but it won't work with me. If you ask me, she's a jumped-up nobody, trying her luck. I'll have to keep my eye on her."

When morning came, the old couple led Constance down to the great hall, to tell her story. As Constance drew near, Lord Allen smiled kindly. But Donegild's expression grew sharp and suspicious. Constance looked from one to the other. She opened her mouth, but no sound came out. How could she tell this woman the story of the Emperor's cruel mother? Surely it would only make her angry – or worse, give her terrible ideas.

Lord Allen smiled again. "No need to explain," he said. "Your kindness speaks for itself. I've heard nothing but good about you in the village. Stay here as long as you wish." Constance looked up at Lord Allen, tears of gratitude in her eyes. But she resolved to steer clear of his mother, if she could.

Lord Allen stayed at the castle for many months. Every day he saw Constance, and every day he admired her more. "Marry me, Constance," he said one day, "I don't know anything about you but I do know that I love you!"

Constance turned pale. "My Lord," she said, "I have loved you since I first saw you. But I am nobody here. If I marry you, people will be angry and suspicious."

"Dear Constance, everyone loves you," he replied. "Your kind deeds have won their hearts, just as your beauty won mine." And so they were married in the castle chapel the very next day. The old couple beamed with happiness and the villagers clapped and cheered. But Lady Donegild watched the ceremony through narrowed eyes. "It won't be long," she said to herself. "Soon I will find a way to get rid of this nobody!"

For a year, all was well. Lord Allen had never been so happy and Constance was happier still. She had a husband who loved her, and she knew that, soon, she would have a baby, too.

Then, one morning, Lord Allen called her to him. "Dearest wife," he said, "I have lingered too long. Important matters call me away. But you will be safe here. My mother will take great care of you."

Constance felt anxious, suddenly. "Very well, my lord," she replied, "but hurry home. The baby will soon be here."

That very night, the baby arrived – a tiny boy. Constance named him Maurice. Lady Donegild seemed delighted. "I must write to my son!" she exclaimed. "The fastest rider in the land will take him my letter. He will be overjoyed with this news." She realized her chance had come.

In a week, the messenger returned. He galloped through the castle gate, his horse's hooves clattering in the cobbled yard. "A message from Lord Allen!" he cried. Donegild rushed forward, trembling in her haste to snatch the letter. She tore it open with a triumphant smile, but she scarcely seemed to read it. After one quick glance, she hurriedly tucked the letter into her sleeve.

"Call the guards!" she shouted. Everyone gathered around to hear the news.

The captain of the guards strode into the yard, his troops at his heels. Lady Donegild drew a letter from her sleeve. "Read this" she said.

The captain read, astonishment on his face. "But my lady," he cried, "how can this be?"

Donegild stepped forward and addressed the crowd. "My son writes that now a child has been born, he is ashamed of having married a penniless nobody. Constance and her son are banished. He never wants to see them again."

"It can't be true!" cried someone in the crowd.

But the captain of the guard strode grimly forward. "It's all here in this letter," he said.

Young and old wept piteously as the guards led Constance and her child down to the beach. A tiny boat lay ready, and Constance climbed in, holding the baby tightly to her, soothing his cries as best she could.

"I came here in a boat with no oars or sails and I am leaving the same way," she said. Even the guards were weeping as they pushed the boat out to sea. Once again, Constance was adrift on a vast ocean, with a meagre ration of food and water. But she knew for the sake of her child that there was only one thing to do. She turned and set her face firmly forward. "It will all turn out for the best," she said.

For days and nights the boat drifted, sometimes floating slowly on calm seas, sometimes scurrying across stormy waves. Constance grew weak and even the baby stopped crying, lying still and exhausted in her lap. But the day came when land appeared. As it drew steadily nearer, Constance felt something stirring in her mind, as if she had seen this place before. Just then, a ship loomed into view. With the last of her strength Constance cried out feebly; she remembered nothing more.

When Constance came to, she thought she was dreaming still. Her father, the King, was leaning over her, gently lifting the baby in his arms. "Constance," he cried, tears falling down his cheeks, "my poor child! How can this be? You have found your way home to us!" That night, in the comfort of her old room, Constance told the tale, her son sleeping, warm and happy, in her arms.

"We heard of the Emperor's death," said her father. "We've been warring with the wicked Empress ever

## The Man of Law's Tale

since. But we never learned what had become of you. Your cruel new husband must be found and punished. Tell us his name and where he lives!"

But Constance shook her head. "I still love him, even if he doesn't love me," she said. "One day, he may change his mind. After all, stranger things have happened. Look how, across all the wide world, I drifted home to you."

Back at the castle, Lord Allen had returned. "My wife and child banished!" he cried, "How could you believe I would order it?" The captain of the guards showed him the letter. "You fool!" shouted Lord Allen, "this is not what I sent. It is my mother's writing – she must have switched the letters."

Donegild laughed when he challenged her. "Prove it!" she said. But late that night, she crept from the castle with all her jewels, never to be seen again.

Lord Allen wept as he paced the castle walls. "I have sent fast ships and riders to find them," he lamented, "but I fear I may never see my wife and child again!"

Years passed. Baby Maurice grew into a boy, as handsome as his father and as kind as his mother. One day, as he played in the palace gardens, he heard a commotion and ran inside to find out what all the fuss was about. His mother came to meet him, pale but smiling. "It's a big day for you!" she said. "A great lord from a distant land has come to visit. You must go to meet him."

"Aren't you coming too?" asked Maurice, wriggling as

his mother washed his face and brushed his hair. "Not now," said Constance, "but we'll see – after all, stranger things have happened."

Maurice ran downstairs and into the great hall. His grandfather sat on the throne, a tall man in a dusty cloak standing before him. The stranger turned and, as he caught sight of Maurice, he staggered back and put a hand to his head.

"Come here, child," he said. "Let me look at you." His eyes scanned the boy's face eagerly, then he sighed. "I thought I had seen a ghost," he said. "You look so like my wife. My own mother banished her, and said I had ordered it. Since then I have searched the world, trying to find her again. But I fear she was drowned long ago."

"Perhaps not, Lord Allen," replied the old King. He whispered to a servant, who hurried from the room and returned, leading Constance by the hand. As Lord Allen caught sight of Constance, he rushed to greet her, weeping tears of joy.

Constance stood still and quiet as he poured out the true tale of his mother's treachery. Then she kissed him tenderly. "Stranger things have happened," she said. "But we must never be parted again." And they never were, until the end of their days.

"Well," said Harry, "that was an honest tale with a happy ending. Let's have another one just like it. You men of learning seem to be good at this tale-telling thing, to judge by the lawyer there.

Now, Parson, I'll take my oath you could tell us a good tale, by God!"

"Bless the man, why does he want to come out with all that swearing?" the Parson murmured, in a fluster.

I must admit, I didn't share Harry's faith in the Parson – we were more likely to be treated to a big old Sunday sermon than an amusing anecdote.

The Wife of Bath must have formed the same idea. "Here we go," she put in, "he'll be preaching to us all before we know it! We'll get quite enough of that in Canterbury, thank you very much. It's not as though we need reminding about our religious duties. We're on a pilgrimage, for heaven's sake, isn't that enough? I'll tell the next tale – it won't be all learning and philosophy, but it will be a right good yarn!"

# The Wife of Bath's Tale

(about a Knight and a Loathly Lady)

"I'll tell you a tale about marriage," said the Wife of Bath, pushing back her huge hat (it was as big as a shield) and scratching her head. "After all, I've been married five times, so I should know about it! Some churchmen think marriage vows should be made once only. But King Solomon and Abraham both had more than one wife, and they're in the Bible, aren't they?"

She grinned around with glee. "All my husbands passed away before their time – what could I do but choose new ones? I'll admit, some were good and some were bad, but I taught each of them a thing or two!" She settled her full skirts over her massive hips with a satisfied smile and began her tale...

Chaucer  The Merchant  The Wife of Bath  The Summoner  The Pardoner

## The Wife of Bath's Tale

**B**ack in old King Arthur's time, this land was full of fairies. Now these pestilential priests and friars have driven them out, crawling all over the place with their prayers and their blessings. But then, they say, you could see the Fairy Queen and her maidens dancing in many a grassy meadow. They had all kinds of powers for good and for ill – but, sometimes, humans made quite enough trouble all by themselves.

One Midsummer's Eve in the castle of Camelot, a crowd of angry villagers burst into the great hall. There were raised voices and pointing fingers. They were there to seek justice from King Arthur himself.

"What is this?" called the King. The crowd parted and a girl stepped forward, dripping wet from head to foot. Water streamed from her long hair and from the damp blanket she clutched around her naked body, making a puddle on the floor. "Justice!" she cried.

"I was bathing in the river, when a knight came along – one of your knights. I'd know him again, anywhere. He saw me in the river, and..." her voice trailed off and she began to sob.

"You need say no more," the King replied, "your distress is clear enough – we can all guess what happened. And we all know the law. A grave assault like this – his life is forfeit."

Then Queen Guenevere stepped forward. "Yes, my lord," she agreed. "We all know the law. But to lose his life – what purpose would that serve? Grant me his life, I beg you."

The King hesitated. The dripping girl clenched her fists and the crowd buzzed with whispers, uncertain which way things would go. At last, the King bowed his head. "He's yours," he said to the Queen, "I know you will see justice done."

Guenevere stepped forward and raised her hand for silence. "Show me the culprit," she said to the girl. With a trembling hand, the girl pointed at a young knight. The crowd gasped. The knight turned red and scowled. The Queen looked at him with disgust. "Come here and receive my judgement!" she ordered.

Slowly, the knight stepped forward and kneeled before the Queen with a sulky air. "By rights," said the Queen in a loud, steady voice, "I could have your head cut off. But what good would that do? Instead, I'll teach you to show women respect. I'll give you a year and a day to find out what it is that women most desire. When the time is up, return here and tell me. If you can't – your neck will feel the cold iron!" She glared down at him as he gulped and stumbled away. "Remember!" she called after him. "What is it that women most desire?"

The knight rode, alone and friendless, halting at each and every place he found to ask his question. As the summer flowers slowly faded and yellow leaves began to fall, he stopped at grand palaces, silent monasteries and remote hunting lodges. As the bitter winds whipped through the bare branches and deep winter snows covered the ground, he stopped at busy inns and market squares. And as the spring flowers put forth their buds and blossoms, he stopped at lonely farms, dank dungeons, and even a pigsty. And everywhere he stopped, he asked the same thing: "What is it that women most desire?"

All sorts of women gave him all sorts of answers. But, try as he might, he could find no two women who agreed. Some said that women loved riches best, some said happiness, some said pretty clothes, some said lusty lovers. Some said women liked to be told they were right; some that they didn't want to be told anything at all. And some said that what women most desired was to be thought sober, sensible and trustworthy.

I'll leave you to judge for yourselves whether any of them were close to the mark!

At this, the Wife of Bath peered around at the other pilgrims, as if challenging them to venture an opinion. No one dared.

"By God," I heard the Pardoner mutter to the Summoner, "I was about to get married, you know, but I think that Wife of Bath has changed my mind. You couldn't put a foot right with a wife like that!"

Luckily she was a little deaf and didn't seem to hear him as she went on with her tale...

A year was almost done, and the knight had asked every woman he could find – rich and poor, wise and foolish, high-born and lowly. But he knew in his heart that he had not found the answer. He sighed sorrowfully and turned his horse for home. He had done wrong and now his life was forfeit. Finally, at the year's end, he could see it was a just punishment.

But as he rode slowly back on Midsummer's Day, on the fringes of a great forest a strange sight met his eyes. Between the trees he glimpsed a band of dancers, glimmering strangely in the low evening light. They had wild, flowing hair and danced with such airy movements, they hardly seemed to touch the ground.

The knight felt a last gleam of hope. "Perhaps these maidens can answer my question!" he thought, and he scrambled from his horse, half running, half stumbling through the trees towards them. But suddenly, before he could get to them, the dancers vanished.

The knight looked around wildly, but he could see no living creature... But what was that, crouching on the grass under a tree? It took him a few moments to realize it was a woman – and what a woman! She looked at least a hundred years old. Dark, sunken eyes glittered out from a mass of wrinkles, and her frame was so twisted and hunched, it was hard to tell whether she was sitting or standing. Filthy rags hung from her and she leaned on a stick almost as bent and knotted as herself.

"There's no way through here, sir knight," she croaked. "Tell me, what are you looking for? Perhaps I can help you. We old folk learn much in our long lives."

"You are very kind," replied the knight, bowing. "My life is forfeit if I fail to answer this question: what is it that women most desire? If you can help me I will be in your debt forever."

The old crone fixed him with her flashing eyes.

# The Wife of Bath's Tale

"Swear to me that you'll do whatever I ask," she said, holding out a gnarled hand, "and I'll tell you what you want to know."

"I swear, truly!" gasped the knight, clutching gratefully at her hand.

"Then your life is saved," said she, hobbling to her feet. "There's not one woman, even Queen Guenevere, who would dare to say me nay. Here's your answer!" And she leaned towards him and mumbled in his ear.

That very night the knight rode back to Camelot with the crone perched on his saddle before him. He found the whole court waiting for him. "You have kept your promise and returned in a year and a day," said Queen Guenevere haughtily from her throne. "But can you give me my answer?"

The knight stepped forward, feeling the eyes of every woman in the room upon him.

"My lady," he said, his voice low but steady, "what women most desire is liberty. They want the freedom to do as they please. You all know this is true. Now, do what you want with me."

Silence fell in the court. There was not one widow, wife or maiden who disagreed. The knight's life was saved. But the silence was broken by a strange scraping sound. The old woman was thrusting her way through the crowd with her stick, dragging herself forward.

"My lady," she cried, "I gave him the answer. In return, he promised to do whatever I asked. Now I will ask him, here before the whole court. Sir knight, will you marry me?"

"Not that!" cried the knight. "You saved my life, I admit it. Take my land, all my possessions, but leave me alone, for pity's sake!" But the old woman shook her head.

"No, sir knight," she said, "I may be old, poor and ugly, but I wouldn't take all the riches of the earth in exchange for what I want. Love me and marry me."

The knight blustered and protested, but there was no way out. He had promised and he had to go through with it.

Perhaps I ought to tell you of all the joy, laughter and feasting at the wedding – but there wasn't any. They were married in private, and after the ceremony the knight hid himself away in shame and sorrow at his loathsome wife.

"Dearest husband," said the crone, as the knight paced the room in angry silence, "is this how King Arthur's knights all act on their wedding days? I saved your life and now I'm your own love, your dear wife. I never did you wrong in any way. What's the matter? Tell me, and if I can I'll try to make it better."

"Make it better!" The knight let out a scornful laugh. "As if you ever could! You're poor and old and foul – is it any wonder I'm upset?"

"Is that all?" she croaked. "Well, I can fix that easily. But don't you think it could be much worse? Is it really so bad that I don't have a great fortune? If I were rich, I might look down on you for being only a poor knight. And would you really wish me young and beautiful? Wouldn't you worry about all the other men who might be after me?"

She laid a wizened hand on his arm. "I can change," she said, looking into his eyes, "but you must choose. Would you have me old and foul, and your true wife forever? Or would you have me young and fair, but never to be trusted?"

The knight stared at her, amazed. As he gazed into her glittering eyes, he remembered the strange, vanishing dancers and her sudden appearance. Now he knew that some enchantment was at work – he must choose rightly to break it. He sighed and paced, wringing his hands as he wondered what to do for the best. But still, he couldn't decide. At last he kneeled before her and humbly replied.

"My lady, my dear wife, I put myself in your hands. You are free to choose as you please – I will be content with whatever you decide."

"You learned your lesson well!" she cried, and before his eyes the thousand wrinkles melted away, the knotted back unbent and straightened and the sparse grey hairs lengthened and spread into flowing tresses. All that remained of the old crone were those shining eyes, now looking out from the laughing face of a beautiful maiden.

"The enchantment is broken," she whispered. "Because you gave me the freedom to choose, we will have the best of both worlds. I will be both young and true – thanks to your gift of liberty! Now, kiss me!"

The knight kissed her, as she had invited him to, and from that moment on they were the happiest couple in the world, because they gave each other both trust and freedom.

The Wife of Bath adjusted her hat to an even more rakish angle than before. "That's the kind of husband I like," she chuckled merrily, "meek, young and lusty – they're the best ones!" And she winked at John, the Priest. The Prioress looked extremely put out.

The Pardoner and the Summoner drew on ahead, discussing something very busily in lowered voices. I thought that perhaps the Pardoner's bride-to-be was about to make a lucky escape.

Riding just behind the Wife of Bath, the Merchant shivered. "God save us all from wives like her!" he mumbled into his beard.

# The Friar's Tale

(about a Man who went to the Devil)

"God bless you with a long and happy life!" the Friar said to the Wife of Bath. "That was a magnificent story and you are a magnificent woman." He smiled at the Wife, while the Prioress crossed herself and raised her eyes to heaven. The Friar grinned. "I think I'll tell the next tale," he said.

"What a... splendid idea," said the Wife of Bath nervously. The Friar laughed.

"I know what you're thinking," he said, "but I promise you, I'm not going to tell some long, boring, moral tale. On the contrary, my tale will be short and silly."

A mischievous grin appeared on the Friar's face. "I'll tell a tale about a summoner, since everyone knows what villains they are."

"Watch it!" said Harry.

"Of course, I'm not saying that our Summoner *here* is a bad man," said the Friar. "I'm only saying that every summoner I've ever met has been a cheat, a vagabond and a scoundrel."

"I won't have you being rude about any of the pilgrims..." Harry began, but the Summoner himself interrupted him.

"The Friar can say what he likes," he said bitterly. "And afterwards I'll have my turn. And I'll show him what it means to be a holy friar, and fritter your life away with wine and women."

"Enough of this squabbling! You'll get your turn," said Harry. "Friar, please begin..."

There was once a summoner who was riding along a road, going about his usual business. That is to say, he was going to frighten some poor old widow, and squeeze some cash out of her. You see, the summoner was a thief and a swindler of the meanest sort. He worked for a bishop, and the Church law was fierce. If anyone broke it they'd have to go to court. And, if they didn't go, there was a stiff fine to pay. So the summoner would accuse innocent people of breaking Church rules, and the poor people would pay him so they didn't have to go to court.

I wasn't being completely fair when I said the summoner was a thief. To do him justice, he was a liar and a blackmailer too.

So, when this summoner met a man riding along the road, naturally, he didn't tell him what his job was.

"I'm a... rent collector," said the summoner.

"And so am I," said the stranger, who was wearing a smart green coat and a tall black hat. The summoner knew a rich man when he saw one, and so he smiled at him graciously.

"I don't know this part of the country," said the stranger. "Perhaps you could show me around? And if

# THE FRIAR'S TALE

you ever come to where I live, do visit my home. I've got a tidy bit of gold and silver stacked away. You're welcome to however much you like."

"I'd love to," said the summoner. "So... where do you live? Just in case I ever come and see you."

"Far away," said the stranger. "But I promise to take you there one day."

"Since we're in the same trade," said the summoner, "do you have any money-making tips? Any little tricks you'd care to pass on?"

"My wages are terrible," said the stranger. "My master's a hard man and my job's not an easy one. But you know what I do?" He lowered his voice. "I trick people in every way that I can think of."

"But that's wonderful!" said the summoner, his face lighting up. "So do I! Of course, I'd starve if I didn't."

The two men rode on in pleasant conversation. They discovered that both of them were cheats, liars and thieves. The summoner had never met anyone so manipulative, dishonest, untrustworthy and deceptive. He was bowled over with happiness. The two men shook hands and swore they'd be friends all their lives.

"I'm so glad I met you today," said the summoner. "Tell me, what's your name?"

"Do you really want me to tell you? Really?"

The stranger shot the summoner a mischievous look, and the summoner nodded.

"I am a devil, and I live in hell," he said. "I'm here on business, to see if anyone has anything to give me. I'm collecting what I'm due – just like you, it turns out."

"But you look like as much like a man as I do!"

"I can take any shape I like. I can appear as an angel, a man, or a monkey," said the devil.

"So, what's hell like?" said the summoner.

"I could tell you," said the devil, "but firsthand experience is so much better than just hearing about something, don't you think?" The devil smiled. "Well, I'm off. I've got business to do, and I've taken nothing all day."

"I'll come with you," said the summoner. He'd never met such a devious person, and he wasn't about to let him get away. "We can go about our business together."

So they rode on, and soon they came across a cart loaded up with hay that was stuck in a ditch. A man sat on top of the cart, swearing at his horse.

"Go to the devil, the lot of you! Horse and cart and hay and all!"

"Looks like that's yours for the taking," said the summoner to the devil.

"Don't speak too soon," said the devil. Just then, the horse pulled and strained and staggered forwards, and the cart jolted out of the ditch.

"Hup hup!" the carter said to his horse. "God bless you, and all his creatures! Well done, lad, that's the way." And the cart rumbled away down the road.

"See what I mean?" said the devil, as they rode on.

"Let me show you a trick or two of my own," said the summoner, keen to show off. "I'm not a rent collector – I lied to you. I summon people to court, and if they don't go, they have to pay. There's a nasty old woman in that house over there. She's done nothing wrong, but I swear I'll get some money out of her."

The summoner rapped on the old woman's door, and winked at the devil. "Come out! Come out!"

The door was drawn back slowly, and an old woman appeared behind it.

"What is it?" she said. She was leaning heavily on a stick, and her face was a dense map of wrinkles. She had bright blue eyes, which looked suspiciously at the young man in front of her.

"I've a bill here to summon you to court," the summoner said, in a serious voice. "If you don't come to answer the charges, you will be excommunicated from the Church."

"But I can't go!" she said. "Look at me! I've been ill, can't you see? The journey would probably kill me! Why can't you give me a copy of the bill? Then my lawyer could go to court instead of me, couldn't he?"

"Fine," said the summoner. "You can give me twelve pence instead, and I'll drop all the charges."

He folded his arms and waited for the money.

"Twelve pence! Well I'm sorry, but I don't have it," the old woman said, scowling at him. "I don't have a single penny in the house. And more to the point, I haven't done anything wrong!"

"If you don't want to give me your money, I'll take your furniture, your clothes – and what about that nice new frying pan you've got?" he said, peering past her into her kitchen.

"Besides, that's not all you owe me for," he went on. "I'm sure I could remember sins in your past that I overlooked at the time…"

"I haven't done anything wrong!" shouted the old

woman. "Just go away and leave me alone!"

"May the devil in hell take me if I let you off," said the summoner.

"You're a liar!" shrieked the old woman shrilly. "Go to hell!"

"Come now," said the devil, jumping down off his horse. "Do you really mean that?"

"Unless he apologizes and goes away," said the old woman, her eyes flashing, "let the devil take him, body and soul, and the frying pan too!"

"I'll have your money, you horrible old hag," jeered the summoner.

"I don't think you will," said the devil. "Your body and soul belong to the devil, and tonight I shall take you to your new home. Hell." Now I could tell you about the torments the summoner suffered, but I don't want to offend the delicate sensibilities of the ladies among us. So let us simply pray that none of us ever ends up there.

# The Friar's Tale

During this story, the Summoner had turned a pale shade of grey. His jaw quivered, and his hands were gripping his bridle as if he was trying to strangle it.

"Friends," he said, with a hollow laugh, "let me tell you a tale. A tale about a friar. For it seems our Friar is quite familiar with hell."

Haven't you heard about the friar who visited hell in a vision? An angel showed him the sights, so to speak. There were terrible, grotesque, horrible things to be seen. But oddly enough, there wasn't a single friar in sight. And so the round, tubby friar turned to the angel.

"I'm glad to see there are no friars in hell," he said.

The angel laughed. "Oh no, there are a more than a million friars here."

At that moment, the devil, Lucifer, stood up. He was as tall as a mountain, with a long, scaly, lizard's tail. From underneath him scurried out hundreds and thousands of tiny friars, running like ants in all directions.

"As you know yourself," said the angel, "friars are often very well padded. That's why Lucifer likes to use them as a cushion."

The Summoner looked at the Friar and laughed once again.

"How horrible!" said the Prioress, looking quite distressed. "I do not like these sorts of stories. They are not good for my digestion. Can't we have a romantic tale? I like those ones much better."

"Well, let's have something light-hearted," said John the Priest. "We can't have the women fainting on us, can we?"

"I agree with the Prioress," said the young Squire. "What about a story of a young man and a beautiful young, delicate lady, who fall in love..."

"Love?" said the Merchant bitterly. "You want to know about love? I'll tell you about love."

# The Merchant's Tale

(about Love, Marriage and Pear Trees)

This outburst was the first we had heard from the Merchant all day. His usual habit was to ride along, staring glumly into space, saying nothing at all. And when he did speak, he had only one subject of conversation.

"Weeping, sleepless nights, despair – I've had them all, just like any other married man," he said.

"Been married long?" asked Harry.

"Two months," said the Merchant, "two long months." He sighed deeply. "It might not sound long, but it feels like a lifetime. My wife is unique in that she has no human feelings at all. After the Friar's story, I think I might have worked her out. I think she must be a devil in human form."

"She sounds like quite something," Harry said. "Why don't you tell us a tale about her?"

"Oh, I couldn't do that," the Merchant replied. "There aren't enough words in the language to describe how diabolical she is. But I will tell you a story. It won't have any romance in it: that would far be too depressing. No – my tale will be about the good things in life. No lovers! No weddings! No women! Instead, I'll tell you all a cheerful story..."

Far away, in the land of Lombardy, there lived a knight whose name was January. He was a happy, cheerful and contented man, because he was a bachelor. His life was one long series of adventures, victories and feasts.

But on his sixtieth birthday, he decided to get married. All day long he spied out of his window or prowled around the town, on the lookout for a pretty young maiden to be his bride.

"I'm not having some old hag," he said to his friends. "I don't want some over the hill, wrinkled-up, half-senile twenty-five year old. Oh no," he licked his lips, "I'm going to get myself a young, innocent wife who will obey my every command."

"Are you quite sure this is a good idea?" his friends asked him.

"Never been more sure of anything in my life," he replied.

Soon enough January spotted a young girl. Her name was May: she was exquisitely beautiful, poor as a mouse, and not a day over sixteen. Within a month they were married. At the wedding feast, January gazed at his new wife with a sly grin. "My love, you look like an enchantment," he said. "Now I shall have true bliss."

"And, er, so, er... shall I," said May.

January sent the guests home as quickly as he could, so he could spend some time alone with his lovely young wife. That night, he fell asleep with his May in his arms,

# The Merchant's Tale

at which point the whole bedroom trembled as January began to snore.

Three tiles fell off the roof, a crack threaded its way down the wall, and even the rats all moved house because of the noise. And next to January, May lay awake staring at the ceiling. And she started to think.

She thought about January's feet with their curling, yellow toenails. She thought about his beard, which scratched her whenever he kissed her. She thought about the wrinkled skin that hung from his neck, and made him look quite a lot like a goat. And she wondered why she had ever agreed to marry him.

At breakfast the next morning, January dribbled his porridge all over his shirt. "I'm so happy, my love," he beamed at May.

"And so am I," said May, and a tear slid down her cheek and into her porridge.

May was not the only person in their household who was miserable. Damian was a young squire who served at January's table, and he was hopelessly in love with May. One day, he poured out all his feelings for her in a letter, folded it up, and slipped it into a silk pouch around his neck.

A few days later, Damian was sick, and May went to his room to check on him. Damian seized his opportunity, and pressed the letter into May's palm.

"Don't tell a soul, please, or I'll be as good as dead," he whispered.

Late that night, while January was snoring in happy oblivion, May ran to the privy and read the letter by moonlight. After she'd read it, she tore it into a thousand pieces, threw it into the privy, ran to her bedroom and scribbled her reply.

*My dearest Damian, I know that you are young and poor, and that I am married, but I don't care. I love you, Damian, and I'd love you even if you had nothing but the shirt on your back.*
*Yours, May*

The next day, the generous lady slipped the letter under Damian's pillow. After Damian had read it, he sprang out of bed, completely recovered.

For the rest of the day Damian whistled as he polished the silver, skipped as he took messages to January, and smiled at everybody in the household. He was completely happy and almost unbearable to be around. Everyone liked Damian, but they just wished he would go back to being miserable again.

Meanwhile, January was enjoying a walk in his

garden with May. January's garden was full of beautiful flowers and fruit trees, and there was only one key to the garden, so January and May could enjoy it in private. January spent many pleasant days in the garden, but one day his good fortune came to an abrupt end: he was struck blind.

"I can't bear it!" he wailed. "Please don't leave me! I love you, May, I really do. That's why I am going to lock you up in this house. From now on, I forbid you to leave my side. You won't be able to do so much as sneeze without me knowing about it."

May was more miserable than ever. She was in love with Damian, but it was almost impossible to see him. Still, they managed to exchange secret messages, and soon they had made a plan to meet in private.

One afternoon, as January dozed and dribbled gently in his chair, May plucked the key to the garden from around his neck. She slipped it to Damian, he had a copy made, and it was back before January had noticed a thing.

The next day, while January and May shuffled towards the garden, Damian opened up the gate, slipped inside and crouched behind a bush.

"My darling wife," said January, as he opened the door to the garden, "You know that I married you out of selfless love, not out of desire. And I hope you will always be faithful to me. You know that if you are, you'll inherit my lands, my house and my goods?"

"How could you think I would ever be unfaithful to you?" said May, bursting into tears. "There's only one thing you can rely on men for, and that's that they never trust anybody."

As May gave a small sob, she caught sight of Damian, coughed twice and pointed to a nearby tree, which Damian scrambled up. And everything would have gone exactly to plan, but it just so happened that January, May and Damian weren't the only ones in the garden that morning.

January's garden was so beautiful that Pluto, the King of the Underworld, and Proserpina his wife, also liked to spend their time there. High up in the tallest tree, they were looking down at the garden, while their train of servants hovered in the air nearby.

"As I was saying, my dearest wife," said Pluto, "it's a simple fact. Women trick men every day. Just look down there. Can't you see that squire, about to steal a kiss from that poor old knight's wife? Well, it's about time that women got what they deserved. I'm going to give the knight his sight back. Ha! And what will his little wife do then? That'll pay you back for all your schemes."

"Then by Saturn, I swear," said Proserpina, "I'll give her a perfect answer. And for her sake, all women will always have a perfectly logical explanation whenever they're caught doing anything wrong. Just watch me, Pluto."

"But she's lying to her husband!"

"That's not the point!" said Proserpina. "There are plenty of women who are faithful and kind. Just because no one writes books about them, you think they don't exist. Well, they do. And you won't get away with

# The Merchant's Tale

slandering them like that. And now, for the sake of all good, truthful, honest women, I'm going to make them wonderful at lying!"

"Well, I've sworn to give the knight his sight back, so I shall."

"And as I am the Queen of the Underworld, the lady shall have her answer," said Proserpina.

Below them, May had led January to the pear tree where Damian was sitting.

"What beautiful fruits," said May, gazing upwards. "I really must have one of those pears. If you lean against the tree, January, I'll climb up onto your shoulders and scramble up."

So January bent down, May scrambled up his back, and Damian helped her into the pear tree.

At once, Pluto gave the old man back his sight. January blinked and looked around. It was a miracle! He had never been so happy in his life! The world was full of joy and – January looked up into the tree, and his jaw dropped. May was sitting on one of the branches, kissing Damian.

"Help! Help! You... little... scheming... liar!!"

"January! How dare you be so rude!" shouted May.

"Rude?! Rude! I just saw you kissing Damian!"

"I've just helped to cure your blindness," said May, "and this is the thanks I get? The doctor said the only way to cure your blindness was to have a fight with a man up a tree. And look, it works. You should be thanking me, not screaming at me."

"But I saw you with my own eyes!"

"A man who's blind can't see perfectly, all at once. The doctor said you might see strange things for a week or two. It's all in your imagination. Honestly January, I'm beginning to wish I'd never bothered trying to help."

"Oh, I'm so sorry," January said softly. "I really thought I saw you kissing Damian. Come down from the tree. I'm so sorry." So May jumped down from the tree into January's arms.

"Thank you my dear. You saved my sight. You're the perfect wife." January was the happiest man alive. He wanted to jump for joy. It was lucky he didn't, as he probably would have broken his hip. Instead, he and May shuffled back to their house, arm in arm.

"Now January," said May, "remember that until your sight recovers completely, you may see a few more strange things, just for a week or two..."

# The Merchant's Tale

"God have mercy on us all," said Harry. "Please don't send any of us a wife like that!"

"Amen to that," said the Miller.

"I'm sure my wife is honest," Harry went on. "She's a nag, a chatterbox, a moaner, a whiner, a gossip and an impudent wench... but she is honest, I'll give her that."

"She sounds just like my wife!" said the Miller. "Go on, tell us more."

"Oh no," said Harry. "I'd tell you, but as sure as the sky is blue, whatever I said would get back to her. I don't have to say who'd tell, but I think we all know who that would be. Women know the market for gossip." He looked over at the Wife, who gave him a smile of unblemished innocence.

"Anyway, I don't have the time to tell you all her faults. If we were on a three year pilgrimage, down to Spain and back, that would be different. Then I could probably fit in a few of them..."

# The Squire's Tale

(about the Five Magic Gifts)

The young Squire was riding a little way ahead of the rest of the pilgrims. With his pristine tunic, embroidered with flowers, and his curly blond hair, he looked as if he'd stepped straight out of a fairytale. Occasionally, he burst into song, and I caught a line or two.

"Oh my dearest lady, oh, you are so fair, oh my lovely darling, you have such nice hair..."

"Oh my sainted aunt," said Harry, "I hope he's not actually planning to sing that to anyone." He rode up alongside the Squire.

"Now Squire, how about a story?"

The Squire gazed off into space, talking softly to himself. "My sweetest darling... you don't look like a bear... No. You're not shaped like a square... No. You smell just like a chair..."

"Squire? Squire?" said Harry.

The Squire jumped up in his saddle. "Oh, I'm sorry, did you say something?"

"Would you like to tell a tale? A romantic tale, perhaps?"

The Squire blushed. "I – I really don't know

anything about love. Or telling stories. But I'll try. It might not be very good... but I'll do my best..."

In a faraway land there lived a brave, noble king named Cambuskan. His daughter, Princess Canacee, looked like an angel. She had pale, luminous skin, wintry blue eyes and coal black hair, and she was known throughout the land for her kind heart.

When King Cambuskan had ruled for twenty years, he gave a great feast and invited all the lords and ladies in the kingdom. In the great hall, the tables were piled up with delicacies. The hall filled with the happy murmur of eating and drinking. A merry evening was underway when the doors burst open and in rode a young knight on a colossal bronze horse.

He jumped down from his horse, strode up to the King, and bowed.

"King Cambuskan," he said, "the King of India and Arabia sends you four magical gifts: a bronze horse, a mirror, a ring and a sword. This horse can take you wherever you wish to go. If you want to soar into the sky like an eagle, ride to the ends of the earth or seek lost cities under the sea, it will do as you command. There is nowhere in the world it cannot go, if you know its secret. He gives you this mirror, which will reveal your true friends and foes. And he sends your daughter this ring," he said, presenting a ring to Princess Canacee.

"When you wear it, you will understand the language of wild birds, and know how to use herbs to cure all pain. Lastly, this sword will strike through the thickest chain mail, and fell the deadliest foe. Nine-headed dragons, fire-breathing monsters, bone-crunching ogres – it can vanquish them all."

He placed the sword at the feet of the King. "The wounds it makes will never heal unless, out of pity, you touch the wound with the sword a second time. Then the wound will vanish as if the blow was never struck."

When he had presented the gifts, the knight sat down to eat, and people swarmed like bees around the beautiful bronze horse.

"Must be fairy magic," said one man.

"It's packed full of soldiers," another said. "They'll jump out any minute now, you'll see."

"He's talking nonsense," whispered the next man to his friend. "It's all just an illusion. The horse isn't really there at all. See?" He swept his arm through the air and yelled as he hit the hard metal.

The knight took King Cambuskan to one side. "The secret to the horse is simple," he said. "There is a pin in the horse's ear," he said. "Simply tell the horse where you wish to go, twist the pin, and you'll be there in a moment. Just twist the pin again to return." The King climbed up into the bronze saddle. He muttered into the horse's ear, and in an instant, he was a thousand miles away, riding silently beneath a glittering vault of stars.

The next morning, everyone was fast asleep – all except Princess Canacee. The sun was streaming in through her window, and she saw the magic ring lying on her windowsill. She slipped it on, dressed, and went out into the castle grounds. As she wandered, she could understand everything the birds were saying. Soon she

heard the sound of crying coming from a tall, white tree. In its highest branches stood a beautiful falcon. It was weeping. When Canacee opened her mouth to speak, her voice sounded strange and wonderful. She was speaking the language of birds.

"Why are you crying?" she asked the falcon. "Come down from the tree and I'll help you." The bird tumbled out of the tree and fell at Canacee's feet. She cradled it gently in her arms.

"Princess Canacee," the falcon said, "when I was young, I was happy and free. I lived on a high rock, and every day I soared through the vast, blue skies. But then I fell in love with a noble falcon. He seemed honest, charming and kind. How was I supposed to know that he was lying?

He swore to me that he loved me, and I loved him for two years or more. But one day, he had to leave. 'Be true to me, as I will always be to you,' I said. He flew away and that very day he saw a vulgar, shabby looking kite on the wing. In a moment, he had forgotten all about me. He fell in love with the kite, and never returned."

The falcon fainted in Canacee's arms, and the princess carried her back to the castle, where she made her a bed lined with blue velvet. She used the ring to make medicine from wild herbs, she fed her sweet foods, and she made her a beautiful, painted cage. Very slowly, the poor falcon began to heal, until one day she was well enough to fly.

And now, I will tell you how the great King Cambuskan went on many curious and amazing adventures on his horse, and how the beautiful falcon won back her love..."

"That was quite a tale," the Franklin said. "You told it quite brilliantly, especially for someone of your age."

"Well, I hadn't actually got to the end," the Squire said.

"I've a son myself," the Franklin went on, "but all he seems to be good for is gambling away his allowance."

"Yes, but, I was just trying to..." said the Squire.

"He spends all his time playing dice with the kitchen boys," the Franklin went on. As he spoke, I noticed that Harry's face was turning an angry crimson.

"I'd give a thousand pounds to see him with some good, civilized friends like you," the Franklin said, "not those nasty young men he spends his time with."

"Brilliant this! Civilized that!" shouted Harry. "You've interrupted the Squire bang in the middle of his story. When you've finished sucking up to the Squire here, you might want to remember that we all have a tale to tell."

"Yes, yes," the Franklin replied. "But as I was just saying to this fine young gentleman..."

"Not another word out of you!" Harry retorted, and the Franklin, wisely, was silent.

"But what happened to the poor falcon?" asked the Prioress. "How did she win back her lost love?"

"And what happened to the King?" asked the Man of Law.

"It seems we will never know," said the Knight, looking at his son. By now the Squire was riding far ahead. He was singing, and some words floated back to me on the breeze.

"Oh, you're pretty as a hare, and you're not called Clare..."

# The Franklin's Tale

(about a Knight, a Fair Lady and a Magician)

"Since you ruined that tale," said Harry, "you can make up for it by telling your own."

"Alright," said the Franklin. "But first, let's have something to eat, and then I'll tell a tale."

"Hmmph," Harry grunted, and we rode on in tense silence until we found ourselves at a decent looking inn. After we'd all tucked into a good supper (and the Friar had tucked into what looked like three good suppers), the Franklin rose to his feet and cleared his throat.

"I have a fairytale to tell you," he said. So we all settled down by the fire, resting our sore limbs, and the Franklin began...

any years ago, on the coast of Brittany, in France, there lived a young, valiant knight who was in love with a beautiful maiden called Dorigen. He performed great deeds to win her heart, but he didn't dare confess his love, because she was a noble lady, and he was only a poor knight.

After a long time, the knight, Arveragus, summoned

up his courage and confessed his love. To his great surprise, Dorigen told him that she loved him too.

"Marry me," he said, "and I will obey you, as any knight obeys his lady."

"And I will be a true wife to you," Dorigen replied.

The pair were blissfully happy for two years, until Arveragus was called across the sea to fight in England. When Arveragus left, Dorigen wept all day and night. She sobbed and sighed and wept and cried and sniffed and snivelled and moaned and moped, and thoroughly enjoyed being utterly miserable.

Her friends tried to comfort her, and one wintry day they took her to walk along the cliffs. Far out to sea, two ships were being tossed about as if they were tiny wooden toys.

"Where is the ship that will bring my husband home?" Dorigen whispered, and looked over the edge of the cliff. Far below her, the waves seethed over jagged black rocks that stood up like giants' teeth. Dorigen sank to her knees.

"Oh God," Dorigen whispered, "why did you make those terrible black rocks? So many ships must have been wrecked on rocks like those. Aren't you supposed to love the world? So why did you make those fiendish rocks? For my husband's sake, I wish they were sunk into hell."

Dorigen's friends led her away from the cliff, and after that, they decided to take her to gardens and rivers, to play games and dance, to distract her from her sorrow.

And so it was, one afternoon in the spring, Dorigen and her friends were whiling away a sunny afternoon in a beautiful garden. After dinner, everyone stood up to dance, everyone except Dorigen, who sat by the side, watching.

Before her stood a knight named Aurelius. He was a fine young man in every respect: talented, handsome, strong, intelligent and rich. And he had been in love with Dorigen for as long as he could remember.

Aurelius had kept his love a secret and never told a soul, although he did sing of his sorrow in songs, ditties, rhymes, roundels and the occasional epic poem that he performed before an audience. And perhaps, at a dinner or a dance, Aurelius may have gazed at Dorigen as if entranced. But Dorigen had no idea of his love.

After the dance, Dorigen and Aurelius strolled through the garden.

"Dorigen," he blurted out, "I wish that I'd gone over the sea, instead of your husband. I wish I'd gone away and never come back."

"What?" said Dorigen.

"There's nothing more I can say," Aurelius said bitterly. "If you love me, you can save me with a word. If you don't, I will die at your feet."

"I would never be untrue to my husband. Take this for my final answer," Dorigen said. But afterwards, she laughed and said: "Aurelius, the day you take all the rocks from the coast of Brittany, I will love you as well as any man. That is my promise, for I know it will never happen."

"Have you no other answer?" Aurelius said.

"None, for I love my husband," Dorigen replied.

Aurelius's face fell. "Then my heart is broken, and I shall die a sudden, horrible death," he said, and turned on his heels.

Dorigen and her friends went home merrily, while Aurelius awaited his sudden, horrible death. When it failed to arrive, he staggered home and fell into his bed in a fever. Meanwhile, Dorigen's husband was on his way home.

"It's his ship!" Dorigen cried, and she ran down to the sea. Soon a little rowing boat was racing over the waves to the shore. As it pushed onto the sand, Arveragus jumped out, ran all the way up the beach, and held Dorigen in his arms.

The lovers' happiness was complete. They spent their days feasting and making merry. And of course Arveragus never imagined that another man could have spoken to his wife of love.

For two years or more, the wretched Aurelius was

sick with fever. His brother looked after him, and tried every kind of medicine, but nothing worked.

One day, he remembered that while he'd been a student at Orleans, he had come across an old book of magic, hidden under some books on a desk in his lecture hall. At once, he saw a chance for his brother to win Dorigen's heart.

"There are magicians in Orleans who can create untold marvels," he told Aurelius. "One could unleash a whirlwind inside a house, another turn a mountain into a mouse, and yet another could unfold a silver castle in the air, and – with just a click of his fingers – make it disappear."

"And what of it?" Aurelius said flatly.

"We can find a magician who will make the rocks vanish, and then you will win your love."

The two brothers set off at once to Orleans. When they arrived at the edge of the city, a man was standing by the roadside.

"Greetings," he called out. "I know why you're here. Don't be afraid, I can help you."

He led them to his house and into a dark room, stacked high with old leather books and strange-looking, complicated instruments.

"Watch," he said. As he raised his hands, a grey mist filled the room. When it cleared, the three men were standing in a forest, with wet leaves under their feet. From behind them came a thunder of hooves, a flock of birds flew overhead, and hundreds of deer came rushing through the trees.

Aurelius heard a tumble and a shout, and two knights on horseback rode past. They veered apart, charged towards each other and their lances met with a crash.

In another moment, the knights and the forest faded away, and Aurelius was standing in a grand hall. In front of him, Dorigen was dancing with a young man. When the pair turned around, Aurelius saw *he* was the man she was dancing with.

The magician clapped his hands. The image crumbled like a butterfly's wing, and the dusty library stood before them.

"Time for dinner," the magician said. "Even lovers have to eat."

They all sat down to a marvellous feast.

"So you'll take the rocks away?" Aurelius asked between mouthfuls.

"For nothing less than a thousand pounds," the magician replied.

"A thousand pounds is nothing," said Aurelius. "I'd give the world for her, if it was mine to give."

That night, Aurelius slept more soundly than he had for years. At last, his happiness was within reach.

This was the month of December, when the world was white with snow. The magician worked night and day, pacing in his library, consulting his tables and scribbling down calculations in his notebooks. At long last, for a week or two, the rocks vanished. When Aurelius saw what had happened, he galloped to Dorigen's castle.

"My lady," he said, "my only love! Although you feel no pity for me at all, I must remind you that once, in a garden, you promised me you would love me. And so, my lady, I must tell you, even though I am unworthy, but you can see it for yourself, and when you do, think of your promise, for, for – the rocks have gone."

Dorigen's face turned white as bone. She felt as if she had been struck. "Impossible," she cried, and she ran home, weeping.

Dorigen was inconsolable. "Alack! Alas! I must surely kill myself this very moment, to save my honour! Alas, for I must die!" She went on in this way for three days, until Arveragus came home.

"What's wrong?" he asked, when he saw her crying.

"Alas that I was born!" said Dorigen. The whole story soon came tumbling out, and when she had finished, Arveragus simply smiled at her.

"Is that all?" he asked.

"By God above, isn't that enough?"

"It may be that everything turns out for the best," said Arveragus. "All I know is that you must keep your word, for an oath is the highest promise that anyone can give."

Straight away, he sent for a maid to take Dorigen to town, to keep her promise, and there, in the busiest street, Dorigen spotted Aurelius.

"Where are you going?" he asked her.

"I was coming to find you, to keep my promise as my husband commanded me," she said, and burst into tears.

Aurelius stood for a few moments without saying anything, as the tears slid down her cheeks. In those moments, he saw there was only one thing he could do.

"Madam, please tell your husband Arveragus that I see his great nobility, and your distress. And that I would rather suffer than harm the love between the two of you. So I shall say goodbye to the best and truest wife that I have ever known."

He walked away, hardly believing what he had just done. It seemed to him that his heart was breaking.

When Dorigen returned home, she told Arveragus everything. His joy was impossible to put into words, and they were true to each other for the rest of their lives.

Aurelius was not so lucky. He'd sold everything he had in the world to pay the magician, and he still owed him more money.

"Here is five hundred pounds," he told the magician, giving him a chest full of gold. "I shall pay you the rest, for I've never broken a promise."

The magician frowned. "Didn't you promise me the sum of a thousand pounds?"

"Yes," Aurelius replied.

"And didn't you win the love of your lady?"

"No, I didn't," Aurelius said.

"Well, why ever not?" the magician asked, and Aurelius told him the whole sad story.

"Dear brother," the magician said, "You and the knight both acted nobly. Now, look at me. I'm only a magician, but who says a man like me can't be as noble as either of you? Have back your money. I release you from your promise – there is no more to pay. Good day to you, sir."

"Now," said the Franklin, gazing around at the pilgrims. "Who was the noblest, do you think?" He looked expectantly at the Knight, but the Knight said nothing.

"Well, I don't know," said the Wife, "I just don't know what all the fuss was about! Honestly, two young men to choose from, both with a fine pair of pins – and all she does is get into a tizzy! That girl was a fool if you ask me."

"Pardon me, but I think you misunderstand the tale," the Knight said solemnly. "Arveragus did the first noble deed, and gave an example to the others."

"Noble deed my foot," said Harry. "What kind of promise was that? Sending his wife off to cheat on him? If that's nobility, you can keep it."

"And as for Aurelius," piped up the Wife of Bath again, "he should have had a cold bath and stopped mooning around. What a drip!"

"What do you think, my young friend?" the Franklin asked the Squire.

"I think that perhaps Aurelius was the noblest," the Squire said earnestly. "He gave away his one true love. He suffered the most."

He sighed and stared into the distance.

"I think you are quite right," said the Prioress. "Aurelius was a most romantic young gentleman. And it was he who made the knight and his lady so happy."

"Happy?" said the Merchant. "Pull the other one! Dorigen had a plan with Aurelius all along. It was obvious! The little witch fooled them all. If you can't see that, there's really something wrong with you."

"Dorigen?" said the Wife. "What do you mean? Don't be ridiculous!"

"Don't you see?" said the Merchant. "She managed to keep them both: Arveragus and Aurelius. She fooled her poor husband. You think Aurelius would send her away like that? I don't think so. She just lied to Arveragus."

"She did not!" said the Wife of Bath. "How could you possibly think that?"

The argument went on and on, and the pilgrims could still be heard squabbling far into the night, as the embers died down in the fire.

# The Pardoner's Tale

(about Death and the Three Wastrels)

Next morning, the pilgrims set out on the road none too early.

"Who's for the first tale of the day, then?" yawned Harry.

"Me!" cried the Pardoner, who looked far more awake than most of us. Harry nodded vaguely at him.

Chaucer   The Prioress   The Pardoner   Harry Bailey

"I can spin a pious yarn better than most of you," the Pardoner began, his bulging eyes glittering at the company. "When I sell my 'holy relics' – worthless rags and old pigs' bones – I make my speeches loud and masterful, spicing them up with bits of Latin to impress the ignorant and piling on the guilt.

'Greed is the root of all evil,' I tell them, while I scoop up their hard-earned coins. I don't care a straw how many widows' children go cold and hungry, as long as I've got cash enough for a cup of wine with a pretty wench!" He shook back his head, his lank, pale hair flopping about his collar. "Here's one of my sure-fire money-spinners," he announced. "Quiet, now…"

Once there were three youths who were the devil's own companions. They drank, they gambled, they swore and they stayed up till all hours of the day and night – they were terrible fellows! One morning, in the small hours, as these wastrels sat in a tavern drinking, they heard the mournful tolling of a bell, carried before a coffin on its way to be buried.

"Here, you," one of the three shouted at a servant, "go and find out who's died."

"No need," replied the boy, "I already know. He was one of your old friends, struck down as he sat drinking this very night. It was done by that sly crook – people call him Death. He stabbed your friend to the heart and was gone before anyone could stop him. You should be careful how you go, with a thug like that on the loose."

"The boy's right," agreed the innkeeper. "Why, this year alone he's already killed men, women and children over in the next village – it's only a mile off. Who knows, maybe he lives there? You'd best be prepared. You might bump into him at any time."

## The Pardoner's Tale

"By God!" bellowed the youth, "this Death needs putting in his place! I swear, I'd like to get hold of him! What do you say, lads? The three of us would be a match for him. Let's track him down! We'll make short work of him!"

The three youths swore that, until they found Death, they would be like brothers. Each promised he would die for the others. And right away, drunk as they were, they staggered off to the next village, shouting and swearing all the way.

Before they had gone half a mile, they met an old man clambering over a stile. He was poor and humble, and greeted them softly, "God save you, sirs."

The boldest of the three answered back. "Who do you think you're talking to, you old cripple? You're so ancient and feeble, how come you're still alive?"

The old man looked straight at him, and spoke. "Because Death won't have me, old as I am," he said gravely. "You shouldn't mock an old man. Someone might do the same to you when you're old – if you live that long. And now, goodbye to you, I must go on."

"Not so fast, old man," said the bold one, "you can't fool us. We all heard you mention that sly killer, Death. You're in it with him, trying to kill us all! Tell us where he is, or you'll pay for it!"

"If you're so keen to meet Death," replied the old man quietly, "turn off along that winding path through the woods. I left him just now under a tree – he'll still be there. See that oak? That's where you'll find him."

Off ran the three youths, straight to the oak tree. There, on the ground, glittering and glinting, lay a massive heap of fine, fat gold coins. Amazed, they fell to their knees by the precious hoard. Suddenly, they'd forgotten all about Death. The vilest of the three spoke up first.

"We're rich!" he said, "I can't believe it! But before we can spend this gold, we need to get it safely home. It's no good by day – everyone would think we'd stolen it. So we'll have to do it secretly, by night. Let's draw lots. Whoever gets the short straw runs into town to fetch us some drink. The other two stay here, on guard. Then, tonight, we carry off the loot."

The youngest of the three drew the short straw, and off he went. As soon as he was gone, the vile one turned to the bold one.

"We're sworn brothers, aren't we?" he said. "I've thought out a way we can both do well from this. We'll get a third of this gold if we all share it out. But what if you and I took half each?"

"Great!" said the bold one, "But how are we going to get away with it? What about our young friend?"

"Easy – it's two against one," the vile one replied. "When he comes back, get up to meet him. You grab his arms, and I stab him in the back. Then we share the cash – we'll have enough to do anything we want!" So the two youths agreed that's how it would be.

Meanwhile, the youngest of the three was still jogging into town. He couldn't keep his mind off the bright gold coins – so precious, so beautiful.

"What if I could have them all to myself?" he wondered. "I'd be the luckiest man alive! But how?" He thought and thought, and at last, it came to him. Poison – that was the safest way. The other two would have to die if he was going to have it all.

When he arrived in town, he went straight to the rat-catcher. "My house has rats," he lied, "a plague of them! I need poison to kill them – the strongest you sell."

The rat-catcher held out a little black box. "The stuff in here will do it," he said. "No creature alive will last for two minutes after eating or drinking this. The smallest taste will kill your vermin."

The youngest one took the box. The rest was simple. He bought three bottles, and poured poison into two of them. Then he filled them all with wine and ran back to the others. Of course, he didn't last long. Just as they had planned, the other two stabbed him to death right away. And when it was done, they sat down to rest.

"I'm parched!" said the bold one. "Let's have a drink. We can bury him later. Lucky he brought us this wine!"

He took up a bottle and took a big swig. The vile one drank, too. You've guessed it – the bottle was poisoned. They died, of course, in horrible agonies. So the three murderers killed each other. They met Death alright, but he got the better of them. He always does.

"So you see," the Pardoner went on, "money is the root of all evil – always was and always will be. Love of gold has caused many a man, woman and child to lose their immortal souls, and all for a glittering bauble, a mere possession, a trashy thing of this world. You are all guilty! You have all blasted your souls with the hideous vice of avarice! You live for the love of gain!"

At this point several of the pilgrims, including myself, began to feel a little uncomfortable. But on went the Pardoner...

"Sinners!" he cried, "Your souls are in peril, but don't despair! I can help you to save them. Here in my pack, I have the holiest relics. Just touching them will lift your souls from the mire of this world and send them soaring closer to heaven." He scrabbled in his pack and brought out a scruffy-looking bottle stuffed with filthy rags.

"For a few coins, a little mere money, you can touch this piece of the very sail St. Peter used when he was a fisherman on the Sea of Galilee. Come on, Harry Bailey, you're the worst of the lot – I've never met an innkeeper who wasn't sunk to his neck in sin. There now, undo your purse! For just fourpence, I'll give you the first chance to kiss this precious relic."

Harry looked furious. "You ugly great fraud!" he roared, "I'd rather kiss your..."

Just in time, the Knight intervened. "Now, now, my friends!" he pleaded hastily, "No need to argue! Shake hands and make it up like good fellows!"

Harry was still glaring at the Pardoner, who was keeping his distance, warily. But, to my great surprise, the Knight persuaded them to shake hands and say no more about it. And so we continued on our way.

# Chaucer's Tale

(about Sir Topaz and the Giant)

"Well now," said Harry gruffly. "Perhaps our next teller would be so kind as to tell a story, not try and hawk their wares at us." He sniffed, and the Knight gave him a sharp look.

"A bit of entertainment's what we need," Harry went on, "not a moral lecture." Before the Knight could interrupt him, he turned to me. "What about you, Geoffrey? You're keeping very quiet there."

Harry fixed me with a stare. "You've always got your eyes glued to the ground, as if you expect a rabbit to jump out of it!" Before I had time to reply, he belted out: "The next tale is coming from this fine gentleman and accomplished poet – Geoffrey Chaucer. He's a funny fellow – he's as round as a barrel, hardly speaks to a soul and half the time he looks like he's a million miles away. Still, I'm sure he's going to tell us a cracking story."

"Harry," I said quietly, "I don't want to disappoint you, but I don't think any of my poems would be quite suitable.

I really don't know any tales," I went on, "apart from one poem I learned a long time ago."

"What's it about?" Harry asked.

"Well, it's got a brave knight in it, and, er, a giant," I said.

"That sounds just the thing," Harry replied, slapping hard me on the shoulder. "Away you go."

And so I took a deep breath and began...

ar far away, beyond the sea
the young Sir Topaz grew.
He was brave and tall and wise
and slightly bendy too.

He had a face as white as bread,
his nose was a bit wonky,
his hair was black and people said
he looked just like a donkey.

At swordfighting and tournaments
he always held his own.
He won first prize at wrestling and
at scissors paper stone.

Now all the ladies loved Sir T:
each night, tucked up in bed,
they dreamed of him the whole night long
(at least that's what he said).

One day Sir Topaz rode his steed
across the countryside.
He galloped headlong through the hills
and as he rode he cried:

"Oh damn, oh cripes, oh lord, oh pants
what am I going to do?
Last night I dreamed a fairy queen
was my one lover true.

In all the world I've never found
a girl who's just quite right,
but when she sees my knobbly knees
she'll love me at first sight."

Brave Sir Topaz rode into a
forest dark and deep.
He lay down on a pile of moss
and promptly fell asleep.

There came a CRASH, there came a THUD;
Sir T awoke and froze.
Before him stood a giant foot

with giant, hairy toes.

From high above a voice boomed down:
"Be gone," it said, "be gone,
or else I'll squash you into jam
and eat you with a scone."

"Well, giant, I would really love
to fight you," Topaz said.
"It really is just such a shame
I left my sword in bed.

I could vanquish you tomorrow
at five o'clock, let's say?
Slay you then, you gangly freak,"
he said, and ran away.

He legged it, scarpered, pranced and skipped
like some demented hare.
As soon as he was back in town
he hid under a chair.

His merry men soon found him.
"Are you alright?" they said.
"You've gone as green as pondweed,
should you be out of bed?"

"Well, I was just preparing,"
he casually replied.
"To fight a smallish giant
he's only ten feet wide."

"So come, my merry minstrels
and tell tales of love and hope,
of castles, dragons, romance,
jelly and the Pope..."

"Stop!" shouted Harry. "If I hear any more of this poetical nonsense my ears are going to explode! I never heard such a load of codswallop, doggerel and general ear-swilling rubbish in all my life!"

So the pilgrims never got to hear the rest of my tale. It was clear I wasn't going to win the storytelling competition, but I was quite happy to fade into the background again...

# The Nun's Priest's Tale

(about a Fox and some Chickens)

"After that piece of drivel, could someone please tell us a decent tale!" Harry said.

"I've got one," said the Nun's Priest, John. He was a peculiar sight. He was tall and handsome and he always had a smile on his face.

His horse, on the other hand, was scrawny, bony and bandy-legged, and each day it managed to look more and more miserable. Every few paces, it tripped over its own feet, catapulting John high into the air. He usually landed in the mud, quite often on his head.

But each time this happened, John just laughed, dusted himself off, pulled the twigs out of his hair, the mud out of his beard and leaped back onto the scraggly beast.

"John," said Harry, "you look like a merry gentleman. And who cares if your horse is a bag of bones? Now, what we'd all like right now is an entertaining tale. To be frank, that last tale wasn't worth a flea's backside. So, make it a lively one, if you wouldn't mind."

And straight away, John began...

In the countryside, a poor widow lived on a farm with her two daughters. She kept a few animals: cows, pigs and chickens; but she had one prized possession, one animal she loved more than all the others put together – her cockerel. He had a jet black beak, a scarlet crown, shimmering golden feathers and legs of the purest azure blue – although it was his toenails that she was most proud of.

"They're as white as the fairest lilies!" she would say to anyone who would listen. The cockerel was called Chanticleer and, every dawn, the whole village awoke to hear his beautiful singing. Everyone agreed that he had the finest voice of any cockerel in the land.

In the yard with Chanticleer lived seven hens – his adoring, loyal wives. The most beautiful of them all was the spectacular Madam Pertelote. Chanticleer adored Pertelote. To him, she was the model of everything a virtuous hen should be: elegant, graceful, charming, beautiful, intelligent, well-read, demure, witty, sophisticated, a good cook, compassionate, wise and kind.

One morning, as the sun rose, Chanticleer sat on his perch, surrounded by his wives. He cleared his throat, breathed in... and an extraordinary sound came out. It wasn't a clear pure note. It wasn't a dulcet tone. It sounded like a frog with a bad case of flu.

"What's wrong with you then?" squawked Pertelote.

"Nothing," Chanticleer mumbled, blushing deeply, looking down at the perch.

"Well, why are you making that awful racket then?" Tact had never been one of Pertelote's most obvious virtues.

"I've had the most horrifying dream," Chanticleer said, turning to her with terror in his eyes. "A portent! An omen! If I can interpret it right, I might just be able to save my life. I dreamed I was walking in the yard, when I saw a monstrous beast. He looked like a hound, but he was bright red, with a black-tipped tail and eyes that glowed like coals. He was going to pounce on me – and kill me!"

"You little coward!" squawked Pertelote. "That's the end of that then. I could never love a coward."

"But it was so real..."

"Don't you realize," Pertelote snapped, "that hens want cockerels who are brave and strong? You might look like a courageous cockerel, but underneath you're about as brave as a tiny little mouse. Afraid of dreams?"

"It was a monster!"

"Dreams and portents?" she screeched, "I'll tell you what's given you your dream. You've been guzzling too much grain, that's what. It's only your indigestion."

"But I..."

"Courage? You wouldn't know courage if it slapped you around the face with a haddock."

"My dear..."

"As I recall," she went on smugly, "it was the philosopher, Cato, who said 'think nothing of dreams'. So, do stop going on about your piffling little daydream and take a laxative."

"But..."

"Oh, alright, I'll find you the herbs myself," she said. "Then – whoosh – it'll all come rushing out like a waterfall. You'll be tickety boo before you know it."

"Madam, I'm sure Cato is very wise," Chanticleer replied (spitting out the word Cato as if it was a piece of rotten grain), "but there are many writers much wiser than him who agree that dreams are very serious portents. Just the other day I was reading a book by, by..."

For a moment, his mind went completely blank. But he recovered quickly, "...by one of the greatest writers of all time," he said. "He told this tale, which proves me right."

"Oh, do get on with it," Pertelote drawled.

"There were two brothers. One brother had a dream that the other brother was about to be murdered. But it was just a dream, so he went back to sleep. Well, what do you think happened the next day?"

"What?" asked Pertelote.

"The other brother was dead, of course! Dead! Dead as a dead doornail! Perished as a poisoned pigeon! Past-it as a parson in a plague pit full of pythons!"

"Really?" Pertelote commented, flatly.

"He had as much chance of survival as a young child at a tea party for extremely hungry cannibals."

"Alright, I get the drift," said Pertelote.

"And if you think I'm going to poison myself with your bizarre herbal remedies, well, you'd better think again. I'd rather go for a dip in the widow's privy, quite frankly."

Pertelote turned away from him and slowly began to

clean her feathers. For a few minutes, there was silence in the yard. Chanticleer detected that the atmosphere had become a little frosty.

"Never mind, my love," he said, "let's talk of more cheerful things. Pertelote? Pertelote? Oh dear," he muttered. He saw that he had gone too far. While there were many dangerous, difficult and deadly things that Chanticleer would face with courage, Pertelote in a rage was not one of them. Some serious grovelling was in order.

"I am such a lucky cockerel. I've got your beautiful face to look at," he said, although at that moment, he was gazing at the mud-clogged end of Pertelote's tail. "Your beauty and grace, my love, are incomparable..."

She looked at him, spat out a piece of grain, and then sidestepped along the perch away from him.

"When I touch your soft wings, I feel so happy and brave," he said. "If only I could get close enough to stroke your splendid feathers. This perch is really too narrow."

He shuffled towards her. She stepped away again.

"With you by my side, my dearest, I'm ready to face the world."

As he spoke, Chanticleer took another step towards Pertelote. Unfortunately, although he was a very handsome cockerel, he was not exactly slim. He swayed, teetered, swayed again, teetered, and then, with a tiny yelp, fell straight off the perch and landed in a heap in the yard.

Chanticleer gulped. He stood up and dusted himself off, looking wildly around him. "I'm a cockerel, not a mouse. Not a mouse," he muttered. He took a step, and then another step. Satisfied that he was safe from lurking beasts, Chanticleer began to walk across the yard. Soon he was strutting around on his tiptoes, whistling. He had forgotten all about his terrible dream.

The whole village could hear him singing as merrily as a mermaid again... And then, all of a sudden, his voice spluttered out. From under a cabbage, Chanticleer had caught sight of a pair of red, glowing eyes.

He was frozen to the spot, and in an instant a bright red fox was before him.

"Gentle Chanticleer, I hope you're not running away from me," said the fox in a voice as smooth as silk. As Chanticleer edged backwards, the fox crept forwards.

"I only wanted to know how you sing so sweetly."

"R-Really?" Chanticleer said, and gulped.

"Your father was the best singer I ever heard," the fox went on. "He had the voice of an angel."

"That's very kind of you," said Chanticleer.

"I don't suppose you can sing like he did, can you?"

Chanticleer blushed. He beamed.

"As it happens, I don't want to boast, but as it happens, I'm actually rather good at singing," he said. "In fact, my reputation stretches throughout the seven farmyards of this village – and beyond."

"Is that so?"

"Is there any particular song you'd like to hear?"

"You choose," the fox said sweetly, and he sat back on his haunches and shut his eyes.

Chanticleer beat his wings, cleared his throat, closed his eyes, stretched out his long white neck, and the fox's jaws snapped tightly round it.

The fox was away in a moment, dragging Chanticleer behind him. As Chanticleer's head bumped along the ground, hitting a bucket, a trough and two logs, the hens flew down into the yard and began to cry.

They gave a moving lamentation for their dead husband and lord. It could have been the burial of an ancient king. No one's grief was more poignantly expressed than that of Pertelote.

"Oh blimey!" she screeched. "What have you done now, you idiot?" Then, not knowing how better to express her loss, she started to run around in small circles, screeching.

In this atmosphere of solemn and profound grief, the widow and her children came running out of the house and spotted the fox streaking through the trees.

"Fox!" they cried. "Get him!"

As they chased after the fox, their dog ran after them, and the cows, startled, chased after the dog. When the cows ran past, the pigs were so terrified that they joined in the chase. Next, a swarm of bees got into a panic and buzzed after the pigs.

"Fox!" they cried, "Fox!"

The stampede was an impressive sight, a sight that would make any fox drop his catch and run to ground. Unfortunately the fox had gone in almost exactly the opposite direction, and the charging animals merely disturbed a couple of ducks on a quiet picnic.

In a shadowy clearing in the woods, the fox stood still for a moment, panting. Chanticleer's heart was thumping like a drum.

"If I were you," rasped Chanticleer, "I'd shout: 'Turn around you fools, I am in the wood, and I am going to have this cockerel for dinner,' right now."

"That," said the fox, "is an excellent..."

Chanticleer broke free from the fox's open jaws and

flew up like an arrow into the trees. He stood on a branch, his heart in his mouth. "I'm alive," he thought. "I'm alive!"

From down below came a wheedling voice.

"Oh Chanticleer," called the fox. "I'm sorry I scared you. I didn't mean to. I have a wonderful plan for us both. Just pop down here for a second and I'll tell you all about it."

"Fox," replied Chanticleer, "exactly how bird-brained do you think I am?"

And the fox slunk home, his black-tipped tail between his legs.

When his tale was finished, John looked up, and saw the Prioress scowling at him, with an expression on her face that could only be described as Extreme Wrath. John coughed, and then continued in a more solemn voice.

"Now, you may be under the misapprehension that this is just some silly story, one that might even seem inappropriate for a priest to tell." The Prioress's scowl deepened.

"But my tale has a very serious moral," John went on, "a moral that applies to all: foxes, men and cockerels."

"What's that?" Harry asked.

"Well," John said, "well. As a, um, a famous saint once said, er, well, er..."

"Never listen to a woman?" shouted the Miller, and the Merchant laughed bitterly.

"You can laugh all you like," the Wife snapped, "but if Chanticleer hadn't been so fond of his pretty little voice, he would never have been trapped by the fox in the first place."

"Whatever the moral, that was a merry tale," said Harry. "But let me tell you, it's lucky that you haven't come on the pilgrimage looking for romance. You're a fine looking fellow, but you wouldn't be getting much appreciation from the lady pilgrims with a tale like that."

"Indeed," John said, and smiled.

We rode along in pleasant conversation for an hour or two, drawing nearer to Canterbury. All of us, I'm sure, were thinking about the dinner and beds that lay ahead.

It almost seemed as if we'd run out of insults to fling at each other and stories to tell, until, by luck, a stranger joined us.

# The Canon's Yeoman's Tale

(about a Wicked Alchemist)

Around five miles from Canterbury, a Yeoman on a sweating horse came into sight, pounding after us. He was poorly dressed for a Yeoman, I thought. They usually did well for themselves, picking up well-paid work here and there, but this one had seen better days.

"I was hoping I'd catch you!" he called, wiping his forehead. "You look a merry company. My master, the Canon, would like to ride with you for a while."

"Welcome," cried Harry. "We'll be glad if you join us – and your master too. But will he have a tale to tell us on the way?"

"Oh, yes," the Yeoman replied, "he can tell you a thing or two. He's not only a Church Canon, he's also an alchemist – he makes gold out of nothing, but not in the way you might think. I spend hours sweating over his fires, mixing this and melting that. But the only gold he gets is from fools who hand it over because they believe his mad ravings!"

As he chattered, a thin man with a stern and haughty face rode up behind him.

"Silence, servant!" he hissed, "it's secret – they won't understand!"

"No, no!" cried Harry, "Go on – tell us!"

"As I was saying..." continued the Yeoman loudly, with an insolent grin. Meanwhile his master threw him a disgusted look and kicked his horse into a gallop, riding off quickly so he didn't have to listen.

"Well," the Yeoman shrugged, "I'll have some fun from him later on! But, in the meantime, I can tell you all something worth hearing..."

The Canon    The Yeoman    Harry Bailey

I've lived with that alchemist for seven years. You wouldn't know it now, but in the beginning I was young and happy – I had smart clothes, clear skin and even a little money. Now my face is wan and greasy from breathing in metal fumes, and I've lost all my money buying alchemy equipment.

It's a slippery science, this alchemy. It's the best way I

know of to empty your wallet and lose your wits. But those alchemists make it look so respectable! All their words sound so learned and mysterious, they seem wonderfully wise! But I tell you, all that glitters is not gold, and those that seem the wisest are often the greatest fools.

The philosopher's stone that turns all metals to gold, that's what alchemists seek. But, if you ask me, it doesn't exist and, for all their skill and cunning, they'll never succeed in making it. So what if they're wise and learned, or poor silly fools like me. They can – and do – spend days and nights solid puzzling over books. But the result's the same, and always will be: they fail.

Keep away from them, I'm telling you! You can spot alchemists from miles off by their foul stink of brimstone and their threadbare clothes. But if you ask them why their clothes are rags, they'll whisper in your ear that it's all a cunning disguise to keep safe the secrets of their art! That's how they persuade fools to invest in their crazy schemes.

No wonder they need more money all the time. They use all kinds of substances for their work, from quicksilver (that's mercury), arsenic, ammonia, brimstone, copper, lead and iron, to lime, chalk, egg white, salt, yeast, ash, clay, dung and urine. They measure them out meticulously: some they mix, some they grind to fine powder on a marble slab. Some they put in flasks and jars made from clay or glass in every shape and size: phials, vials, crucibles, alembics – I needn't list them all. Some they heat in furnaces or fires of wood or coal to soak, distill, sublime, pulverize, redden, whiten, combust, fuse, coagulate, amalgamate – don't ask me the details, I just do what I'm told.

And then do you know what happens? More often than not, the pot explodes with a massive bang, blasting holes in the walls and floor and scattering the contents all over the place. Each alchemist blames the others and they all despair at the wasted work. One says it was left

on the fire too long, another that the bellows weren't operated properly (which makes me scared, as it's my job to work the bellows).

"You fool!" cries another. "Idiot, you didn't prepare the compounds properly!"

"No," says a fourth, "it was because the fire was made from the wrong type of charcoal – I'm telling you, it was that and nothing else!"

I never know what went wrong – but I do know it causes endless grief.

"Well," says my master, "I'm convinced that the pot was cracked before we started – but never mind. Let's do what we always do – sweep up the pieces and start again. We mustn't waste anything."

So I sweep it all up into a heap, then I put it through a sieve and pick through the bits.

"Look," says one of them, "some of our substances are left, though we've lost a lot. We must raise cash to buy some more. I know it didn't work this time, but next time it might be fine." But it never is – each time they try, they fail, and go a little crazier. You'll see I'm right by the time I finish my tale.

There's one alchemist I know whose falseness and cunning are infinite. There's no one in the world to compete with him for lying. He wraps himself up so cleverly in his expert terms that he can make anyone believe him – except, maybe, for a fellow alchemist.

He's cheated many a man before now, and yet folk ride miles to seek him out and make his acquaintance, never dreaming of his deceptions. I'll tell you all about them, if you care to listen. But in case you think it's my master I'm talking about, then I'll set you straight right now. This one is a hundred times more cunning and deceitful.

In London, there was once a priest who had a comfortable life. He lodged in the household of a kind woman who gave him good food and fine clothes and wouldn't take a penny for them, though he had plenty of spending money. One day this priest had a visit from an alchemist. He wanted to borrow money.

"Lend me some gold – for just three days," he asked. "Then I'll pay you back. I give you my word."

The priest gave him the money; the alchemist thanked him and went on his way. In three days, on the dot, he gave back the money. The priest was very pleased.

"I don't mind lending a man a few coins – or anything else I have – when he keeps his word so promptly," he said.

"I'd never let you down!" the alchemist returned. "But now, my friend," he added, "you've been so kind to me. If you like, I'll show you some of the secrets of my art. You'll see wondrous things," he promised.

The priest was delighted. Foolish priest! He had no idea who he was dealing with, nor of the harm coming his way. Wicked alchemist! He was about to betray someone for the hundredth time.

"Here, you!" said the alchemist to the priest's servant, "get me some quicksilver (you know, mercury) – two or three ounces will do – some coal and a bowl of water. That's all I need."

When the laden servant returned, the alchemist took a crucible and a glass vial from the folds of his robe.

"My dear friend," he said, "I trust this to your hands. Take this vessel and measure in just one ounce of mercury. Before your eyes, I'll turn it to solid silver, simply by adding this precious powder. But I don't share my secrets with everyone – so send out your servant while we work."

Behind closed doors and shuttered windows, the priest and the alchemist went to work. They put the coals on the hearth, set the crucible on the coals, and lit the fire. They blew on it till it glowed red-hot. The priest sweated and trembled from the heat and excitement. Then the wily alchemist cast on his 'precious' powder – chalk dust or ground glass if I know anything – but he stayed cool. He had something else up his sleeve – a special stirring stick, in fact.

It was cunningly crafted, the middle hollow, the gap filled with one ounce of solid silver, stoppered in with a plug of wax. You can guess how it worked – as he stirred the boiling mixture, the wax melted and the silver slid out, into the crucible.

"Pass the tongs," cried the alchemist, "time to pour out our silver!" And with the priest's help, he tipped up the crucible into the bowl of water. Clouds of steam billowed up with a fizz and a hiss. When the air cleared, the priest peered down into the murky water.

"It's quite safe!" said the alchemist. "Go on, put in your hand and feel around – you'll find a piece of solid silver at the bottom."

And of course he did. They went to a goldsmith and had it tested – it was pure, as the alchemist knew it would be. Who could be happier than the foolish priest? He laughed, he jested, and he was all on fire to learn the secrets of this sorry science.

"Sell me your powder, for the love of God!" he cried, "I'll pay whatever you ask, if you let me have it."

"Well," said the cunning alchemist, "it'll cost you dear, but as we're friends... say forty pounds!"

No sooner said than done. The priest fetched the money and paid for the worthless powder. The alchemist went on his way – strangely enough, the priest never saw him again. And whenever the priest tried to make silver again, of course he failed.

"The poor priest!" exclaimed the Parson, as soon as the Yeoman had finished. "To be so dreadfully deceived by someone he trusted! As for the alchemist, I have seen men stoop to such deeds because of terrible poverty, but I'm sure he regretted deceiving his friend for the rest of his life."

"I wouldn't count on it!" replied the Yeoman. "And talking of lifelong regrets, I suppose I should catch up with my master the Canon, or I might have to find another, even harder profession than alchemy. Farewell all!"

The Parson looked regretfully after the Yeoman as he cantered off. "I shall pray for him tonight," he said. "No man should follow a path he doesn't believe in."

"True, Parson," the Doctor agreed, "But there are some great philosophies that baffle the foolish, while they enlighten the learned. Alchemy may be one, for all I know of it. But certainly medicine is such a science. To be a great doctor, one must master the knowledge of the humours, astronomy, surgery, drugs, medicines and a hundred other things. One must read the writings of all the great doctors: Hippocrates, Galen, Avicenna, Averroes, Gilbert the Englishman..."

Harry reined back his horse discreetly and let the Parson and the Doctor ride on together at the head of the procession, deep in conversation.

"Well, friends," he called to the rest of us, "I don't know a lot about science and philosophy, but I do know that was a merry interlude. Yet I think it's as well that the Canon and his Yeoman took their leave. We might all have found ourselves persuaded out of a few pennies if we'd spent more time with them!"

# The Manciple's Tale

(about Apollo and the White Crow)

As we came to Harbledown, just a couple of miles from Canterbury, Harry Bailey piped up again.

"Come on, you lot!" he cried. "Get a move on! One of you, wake up that Cook over there, and tell him it's time for his tale. Look, he's fast asleep in his saddle! Wake up, Cook!" he called. "What's wrong with you? Did you overindulge at the inn last night?"

Roger the Cook raised his drooping head slowly and gave a large belch. His bloodshot eyes peered out at Harry from an ashen, haggard face.

"I can't work it out!" he mumbled. "For some reason I feel rather tired – I've no idea why." He tugged at the tatty bandage on his leg, pulling it over his huge, weeping ulcer, and then began to scratch one armpit.

"Well, Cook," the Manciple broke in, "if it will help, I'll take over the tale-telling for you. You really don't look well – your face is pale, your eyes are bleary and, phew, your breath stinks like a pig's! For goodness' sake, keep your mouth closed, or better still, don't ride quite so close to me. That's much better!"

# The Manciple's Tale

The Manciple winked at the rest of the company. "I'll tell you a tale my mother taught me. 'Son', she said, 'many a man's lost his job by opening his mouth and saying too much. But speaking too little will never annoy the boss. Keep your tongue firmly shut in behind your teeth at all times, and remember this story,' she used to say.

That's good advice, you know. I never tell my employers anything if I can help it – especially about my own little enterprises. That's the only way I stay ahead of them, even though they're all cunning lawyers. Silence is the best policy."

And with that the Cook, now fast asleep again, gave a loud snore, and the Manciple began...

When the god Apollo lived on Earth, he was the best archer in the world. He could play every kind of musical instrument too, and his singing voice was a joy to hear. He was also the handsomest man the world has ever seen – and noble, good and worthy as well. He was the perfect flower of manhood.

Now, in his house, Apollo had a crow, which he kept in a cage. This crow had snow-white feathers and sang better than any nightingale. It talked and chattered just like a jay, telling stories and swapping news with everyone who came to the house.

Apollo also had a wife, whom he loved dearly. He did everything he could to please and cherish her, but deep in his heart, he feared she might love someone else. Of course, he loved plenty of other women, as the gods always do. But, all the same, he watched his wife jealously, night and day.

Take any bird and put her in a cage – do your best to give her the daintiest food and cleanest water. But even if the cage is made of gold, the bird would rather, twenty thousand times rather, be in a cold, damp forest eating worms and drinking from a muddy puddle. Every time she can, the bird will try to escape, because the one thing she wants is freedom.

And so the day came when Apollo's wife, tired of her husband's jealousy, found herself a lover. He came to the house one day when Apollo was away. And from her cage standing in the hall, the white crow saw it all. But she said nothing.

When Apollo returned, the crow let out a long, loud laugh. "Why, crow," said Apollo, "what kind of noise is that? You always sing so beautifully to me – you know I love to hear your voice."

"Apollo," cried the bird, "you're a fool! Despite your skill and your good looks, despite your music and your singing, despite all your jealous watching, you're still a fool. Your wife has a lover. I saw them together right here in your house."

Apollo turned away, his face dark with anger. His heart swelled with a murderous rage. His hands moved swiftly: he caught up his bow, fitted an arrow and shot his wife through the heart. She fell down, dead at his feet. Then, too late, he saw what he had done. He went through the house like a storm and smashed his bow, his arrows and his musical instruments. Then he turned on the crow.

"Traitor!" he cried. "It was your wicked tongue that caused all this! Alas, my poor wife! My dear delight! Always so loving and so true – you never betrayed me, yet I struck you down in anger! Where was my mind, my good sense? Oh, how could I be so quick to think the worst of you, without good reason?

And now, crow, you'll pay for your false and treacherous tongue. I'll take away your nightingale's song and your white feathers, and you'll never speak again. You and all crows after you will be black, to show your treachery. You will croak and screech in the storm and rain, so everyone knows it was through you my wife was killed."

And Apollo did just as he said. He pulled out the crow's white feathers and made her black, took away her song and her speech, and slung her out at the door with a curse. And so, all crows now are black and squawking. But they're also free.

"Well," said the Manciple, "that's how the story goes. But, of course, it's not about freedom at all. The real lesson is that you should always be careful what you say – especially to anyone important. That's what my mother always taught me. To keep quiet!"

"Quiet, be bothered!" exclaimed the Wife of Bath. "That crow knew exactly what she was doing. All she had to do was get Apollo angry, then she'd get thrown out of the house, and be free. I don't care if he was supposed to be a god, men are all the same. Hit their pride and they just can't help themselves. That crow knew what she was about, I tell you."

"I don't know about the crow," joined in the Shipman in a menacing voice, "but at least Apollo's wife got what she deserved. There's no room for mercy in a case like that. Unquestioning obedience, that's what a wife owes her husband!"

"Fiddlesticks!" replied the Wife of Bath. "Her only mistake was being found out. Back me up, Madam Prioress! We can't let these men get away with all this nonsense!"

Madam Eglantine sniffed disapprovingly. "I couldn't possibly condone marital disloyalty," she replied a little reluctantly, "but I've often heard it said that love conquers all. I believe some people can behave quite foolishly when it comes to the one they love." She held up her little dog and planted a delicate kiss on its nose. "You agree, don't you, my poppet?" she crooned, tickling it under the chin.

"Well, pilgrims," called Harry Bailey loudly, "we can disagree on the meaning of the tale, but let's all agree that it was well told!"

Silence fell. The evening was drawing in, and as we rode quietly on, we could see Canterbury Cathedral coming slowly into view against the dusky sky, its delicate towers pointing up to heaven like a prayer.

# The Epilogue

(about Why there aren't any more Tales)

"My friends," Harry boomed, breaking the silence, "we're almost there. We'll make it to the inn by nightfall – there's just time for one more tale. How about you, Parson? I hope you're not going to spoil our fun. By the look of you, I'd say you'd be able to tell us some grand tale with a weighty theme. So, out with it! Let's see what you're made of."

"Well," replied the Parson regretfully, "I certainly can't compete with the tales we've heard so far. I won't say they weren't enjoyable – instructive even, some of them. But hardly suitable material for a man of the cloth like myself, I'm afraid."

"But you promised us!" said the Wife of the Bath.

"Besides, 'cat, sat, mat' is about the best rhyme I can think of," the Parson went on. "No, no, I'd be sure to disappoint you."

"But Parson, we all agreed that we would each tell a tale," said Harry sternly.

The Parson paused for a few moments, thinking deeply. "Well, if the Lord will be my guide, I think I can tell you a moral tale – not one of your stories, you understand, but a tale with a few bare words of truth."

## The Epilogue

"That's a fine idea," said Harry, looking a little less enthusiastic than he sounded. "We came on a pilgrimage, after all. Who says we can't listen to a serious tale? Parson, you shall have an audience, just like everyone else here. And since our journey is drawing to a close, it's only fitting to end with something solemn. Get us in the mood to pay our respects to St. Thomas tomorrow, so to speak."

The tale began, and I started to listen, as the Parson told of priests and virtues and vices (there were many more vices than virtues, I noticed). It was hard going, so I decided I'd let my eyes rest for just a moment...

"Hell!" The shout jolted me awake. "Hellfire and damnation!" He shouted again. It was the Parson, I realized, red in the face, telling us about the everlasting punishments awaiting sinners. He was still in full swing. The sun was now setting, and there was a chill in the air, but my eyes kept on sliding shut...

"...that is the only path to tread if you are to be saved from the pains of hell," the Parson went on. "Through penitence and humbleness and lowliness, for the sake of Jesus Christ, Amen."

I rubbed my eyes and looked around, realizing I'd slept through almost the entire tale. But the Parson's last words echoed in my mind. Penitence, lowliness, humbleness. I thought of all the tales I'd heard on the road from London. They didn't seem very penitent or lowly, or humble. But there were some great stories, told by real characters, and I knew that I could make a fine, funny book of them all. With a pang of guilt, I mumbled a quick prayer. Dear God, I muttered, please excuse these tales that I am going to record. Especially the Miller's. Oh yes, and the Reeve's. Not to mention all the poems I've already written, which may not have been, well, exactly moral. I'll write some tales of saints next to make it up to you.

"Well, here we are," Harry said, beaming. "This is Watling Street, and that place on the corner, my friends, is the first inn in Canterbury. Not a patch on my own place, of course," he muttered to me as he rode over to greet the innkeeper.

The journey was over. Of course, there was still the ride back to London, and more tales to be told. But I had some private government business to attend to in Canterbury, and it might take days. The pilgrims would have to make their way home without me. So, as they slid down gratefully from their horses, massaging their tired legs, I slipped off quietly into the darkening streets of Canterbury...

# About Geoffrey Chaucer

The author of *The Canterbury Tales*, Geoffrey Chaucer, led a varied and eventful life during one of the most turbulent periods of British history. He was born in London around the year 1340 as the son of a successful wine merchant, and he grew up in a comfortable family home near the River Thames. He lived in London for much of the rest of his life.

Geoffrey Chaucer probably left home to start work in his teens, as boys often did then. He was a page (a junior attendant) for the Countess of Ulster, and he would have accompanied his mistress on journeys all over England, learning how to behave around nobles and professional people, as well as those lower down the pecking order.

In 1359, he became a soldier in the King's army and took part in an English invasion of France. But all did not go well. The young Chaucer was captured and held to ransom. He was soon released, but left army life soon after. Luckily, he had made some useful contacts, and by 1360 he was working as a messenger, carrying top-secret royal documents across England and even to France, Spain and Italy. He probably picked up some French and Italian on these missions, and he may have had extra duties – negotiating or even spying. Chaucer continued to make mysterious journeys 'on secret business of the King' at various points in later life, even when he had other jobs.

In 1366, he married a royal servant named Philippa, and soon secured a more permanent position as a squire or valet in the household of King Edward III. This would have involved doing various duties for the King around the court, the country and sometimes abroad. Once again, Chaucer's people skills and languages would have been invaluable.

Chaucer may also have trained as a lawyer at this time, acquiring useful legal knowledge. This stood him in good stead when, in 1374, he took a job as a London customs official, collecting taxes on goods being exported by ship. He was so good at this, he received a special royal reward. In 1377, King Edward died and was succeeded by Richard II, who also came to value Chaucer as a royal servant. But violent and bloody scenes in London during the Peasants' Revolt in 1381 may have put Chaucer off life in the capital. King Richard, helped by some of Chaucer's fellow customs officials, managed to calm the rioters. It's not known what part Chaucer played but, very soon afterwards, he gave up his London job and home and moved out to Greenwich, becoming a Member of Parliament for Kent in 1386.

Chaucer had probably been writing in his spare time for years, but it was around this period that he was working on *The Canterbury Tales* – and attracting great praise from other poets. But writing didn't pay, and the royal reward was modest. So in 1389 he took a job as Clerk of the King's Works, organizing building and repairs at important royal properties. One day in 1390, on his way to visit a royal manor, Chaucer was set upon by a gang of thieves, robbed and beaten. Although the thieves were later caught, Chaucer gave up this job and took one looking after royal forests.

In 1399, King Richard was deposed and murdered and a new king, Henry IV, seized the throne. This was bad news for some of King Richard's supporters. But luckily Chaucer was also on good terms with the new king – he had written a moving poem about Henry's mother years before.

That same year, Chaucer moved back to London to live in a house right next to Westminster Abbey, but he died soon afterwards and was buried in the Abbey. The area near his tomb later became Poet's Corner, where the most celebrated British writers are buried. Geoffrey Chaucer – soldier, diplomat, MP, civil servant, spy and poet – was the first.